Nine Lives

By Danielle Steel

NINE LIVES • FINDING ASHLEY • THE AFFAIR • NEIGHBORS
ALL THAT GLITTERS • ROYAL • DADDY'S GIRLS • THE WEDDING DRESS
THE NUMBERS GAME • MORAL COMPASS • SPY • CHILD'S PLAY
THE DARK SIDE • LOST AND FOUND • BLESSING IN DISGUISE • SILENT NIGHT
TURNING POINT • BEAUCHAMP HALL • IN HIS FATHER'S FOOTSTEPS
THE GOOD FIGHT • THE CAST • ACCIDENTAL HEROES • FALL FROM GRACE
PAST PERFECT • FAIRYTALE • THE RIGHT TIME • THE DUCHESS
AGAINST ALL ODDS • DANGEROUS GAMES • THE MISTRESS • THE AWARD
RUSHING WATERS • MAGIC • THE APARTMENT • PROPERTY OF A NOBLEWOMAN
BLUE • PRECIOUS GIFTS •UNDERCOVER • COUNTRY • PRODIGAL SON
PEGASUS • A PERFECT LIFE • POWER PLAY • WINNERS • FIRST SIGHT
UNTIL THE END OF TIME • THE SINS OF THE MOTHER
FRIENDS FOREVER • BETRAYAL • HOTEL VENDÔME • HAPPY BIRTHDAY
44 CHARLES STREET • LEGACY • FAMILY TIES • BIG GIRL
SOUTHERN LIGHTS • MATTERS OF THE HEART • ONE DAY AT A TIME
A GOOD WOMAN • ROGUE • HONOR THYSELF • AMAZING GRACE
BUNGALOW 2 • SISTERS • H.R.H. • COMING OUT • THE HOUSE
TOXIC BACHELORS • MIRACLE • IMPOSSIBLE • ECHOES • SECOND CHANCE
RANSOM • SAFE HARBOUR • JOHNNY ANGEL • DATING GAME
ANSWERED PRAYERS • SUNSET IN ST. TROPEZ • THE COTTAGE • THE KISS
LEAP OF FAITH • LONE EAGLE • JOURNEY • THE HOUSE ON HOPE STREET
THE WEDDING • IRRESISTIBLE FORCES • GRANNY DAN • BITTERSWEET
MIRROR IMAGE • THE KLONE AND I • THE LONG ROAD HOME • THE GHOST
SPECIAL DELIVERY • THE RANCH • SILENT HONOR • MALICE
FIVE DAYS IN PARIS • LIGHTNING • WINGS • THE GIFT • ACCIDENT
VANISHED • MIXED BLESSINGS • JEWELS • NO GREATER LOVE
HEARTBEAT • MESSAGE FROM NAM • DADDY • STAR • ZOYA
KALEIDOSCOPE • FINE THINGS • WANDERLUST • SECRETS
FAMILY ALBUM • FULL CIRCLE • CHANGES • THURSTON HOUSE
CROSSINGS • ONCE IN A LIFETIME • A PERFECT STRANGER
REMEMBRANCE • PALOMINO • LOVE: *POEMS* • THE RING • LOVING
TO LOVE AGAIN • SUMMER'S END • SEASON OF PASSION • THE PROMISE
NOW AND FOREVER • PASSION'S PROMISE • GOING HOME

Nonfiction

EXPECT A MIRACLE: *Quotations to Live and Love By*
PURE JOY: *The Dogs We Love*
A GIFT OF HOPE: *Helping the Homeless*
HIS BRIGHT LIGHT: *The Story of Nick Traina*

For Children

PRETTY MINNIE IN PARIS
PRETTY MINNIE IN HOLLYWOOD

DANIELLE STEEL

Nine Lives

A Novel

Delacorte Press

New York

Published in the United States by Delacorte Press, an imprint of Random House, a division of Penguin Random House LLC, New York.

DELACORTE PRESS and the HOUSE colophon are registered trademarks of Penguin Random House LLC.

LIBRARY OF CONGRESS CATALOGING-IN-PUBLICATION DATA

Names: Steel, Danielle, author.
Title: Nine lives : a novel / Danielle Steel.
Description: New York : Delacorte Press, [2021] |
Identifiers: LCCN 2020012001 (print) | LCCN 2020012002 (ebook) |
ISBN 9781984821430 (hardcover) | ISBN 9781984821447 (ebook)
Classification: LCC PS3569.T33828 N56 2021 (print) |
LCC PS3569.T33828 (ebook) | DDC 813/.54—dc23
LC record available at https://lccn.loc.gov/2020012001
LC ebook record available at https://lccn.loc.gov/2020012002

Printed in the United States of America on acid-free paper

randomhousebooks.com

2 4 6 8 9 7 5 3 1

First Edition

Book design by Virginia Norey

To my brave, wonderful children,
Beatie, Trevor, Todd, Nick,
Sam, Victoria, Vanessa,
Maxx, and Zara.

May you be brave in your losses and your wins,
make wise choices,
and be protected in the risks you take.

May you have happy lives
and be blessed,
lucky, and protected, always.

I love you so much!
Mom/d.s.

Nine Lives

Chapter 1

Mary Margaret Kelly, Maggie, had lived on four military bases by the time she was eight years old. It was the only life she knew, and she liked it. Her father, Kevin, was an Air Force test pilot, and had been decorated for the missions he flew in Vietnam. Her paternal grandfather had been a Navy pilot in World War II.

Maggie worshipped her father. He was handsome and tall and funny. She loved watching him fly planes, although she knew it scared her mother. Nothing scared her father. He was very brave, and he always told Maggie to be brave too. She tried to be. Her brother, Tommy, also tried to be. He said he was going to be a pilot one day like their dad. Maggie was five years older than Tommy, and she helped her mom take care of him when she was busy. Emma was a nurse before Maggie was born, but she stayed home with the kids now, and she always had a lot to do. The Air Force gave them a good life. Her father was a squadron leader and flew training missions. They moved to a new base in Nevada when Maggie turned nine. Her mom didn't like it. It was hot most of the time, except at night, and she said that their dad's missions were going to be more dangerous now, but she didn't say why. Maggie heard them arguing about it sometimes. But her dad loved what he did. His eyes and his whole face lit up whenever he talked about flying. He loved everything about planes.

They'd only been there for three months when Maggie's dad went out on a routine training mission. He kissed Maggie in her bed early that morning before he left. He kissed Tommy, who was sound asleep. Emma got up and watched him from the kitchen window while he drove away. By the time Tommy and Maggie were having breakfast, two men in uniform knocked on the door, came in, and sat in the living room with their mother. Emma didn't make a sound. She just sat there, sobbing quietly, so her children couldn't hear her. After a while the men left.

She told Maggie and Tommy afterwards that their dad had died. She said his plane had malfunctioned and spun out of control. The officers told Emma that if Kevin Kelly hadn't been able to stop it, no one could have.

Three days later, Maggie and Tommy went to their father's funeral. Years later, Maggie could still remember how terrible she had felt, and how impossible it was to believe that her dad would never come home again. The men in his squadron had folded the flag on his casket and handed it to her mother, who had clutched it to her chest with her eyes closed. Maggie had thought she would faint, but she didn't. Maggie kept telling herself to be brave the way her father had told her to be. And she was, braver than she ever thought she could be. She took care of Tommy when her mother stayed in bed and cried all the time after that. Emma hardly ever got up, and Maggie cooked dinner for them.

They went to stay with Emma's parents in Oklahoma for a while, then they came back and moved off the base to Las Vegas. It was the first time Maggie had lived among civilians and gone to a local school. Emma got a job as a cashier in a casino. She didn't want to go back to nursing, she said it had been too long. They stayed in Las Vegas for six months, living on her salary and their dad's pension. After that, they moved to three different states, and finally made their way to Miami, where Emma got a better job at a resort hotel, working as a manicurist in the spa. She lived a quiet life, and never went out on dates, until she met Harry Sherman.

Maggie was fourteen and her father had been dead for five years when Emma met Harry at the resort in Miami where they both worked. He was the catering manager. He wasn't handsome like Maggie's father. He wasn't exciting. He wasn't a hero and didn't fly planes, but Maggie's mother told her that wasn't important. What they needed was a man who wasn't going to risk his life every day when he went to work. She told Maggie that if her father hadn't been in love with the thrill of flying planes, he'd be alive today. He could have been anything. A carpenter, a plumber, a teacher, a contractor, but instead he loved danger. Every time Tommy said he wanted to fly planes too when he grew up, Emma told him, in a harsh voice, that he'd better think of something else to do if he didn't want to kill himself. They learned not to talk about their father, or flying.

Harry was a decent man. He was quiet, serious, he didn't laugh or tell funny stories like their dad, and he didn't talk to her or Tommy much. But their mom said he had a good job. They moved into an apartment together a year after they met. Their mom told them that she and Harry were engaged. They got married a month later.

Maggie was fifteen when they got married at city hall. The four of them had lunch at a restaurant afterwards. Harry went to work as usual that night, there was a big convention in town. He was nice enough to them, and Maggie didn't mind him. He had no children of his own, and he tried to be a father to them, but he always worked until late at night, running the catering side of the conventions at the hotel. Emma seemed happy with him, but her eyes never lit up the way they had when she heard Kevin drive up or when he walked into the room. Her life with Harry was different. They both worked hard, and Maggie and Tommy were home alone a lot of the time until their mom came home from work. Sometimes Maggie had cooked dinner for herself and Tommy by then. They weren't a family the way they had been when their father was alive. They didn't do things together or have fun, they just lived in the same house. And they knew Harry would come home from work every night. Nothing he did was dangerous, and in time, the look of panic left her mother's eyes. Harry wasn't glamorous or exciting, but he was reliable.

Harry sat in front of the TV when he came home at night and drank a few beers. He stayed up late, and was still asleep when they left for school in the morning. He never had anything to say to them anyway. He told Emma he wasn't used to kids. Once a week, he would give Maggie a crisp twenty-dollar bill, and tell her to go to a movie with her friends, or buy something. He bought Tommy a football once, but didn't have time to play with him. The weekly twenty-dollar bill was the only real contact Maggie had with him. Her mother seemed like a different person now, as though something inside her had died when their father did.

When Maggie was sixteen and Tommy eleven, a year after Emma and Harry got married, Harry was transferred to a bigger hotel in Chicago that was part of the same chain. It was a better job, with more money and more responsibility. Emma wasn't happy about it. She said they'd never see him. He'd be working all the time. They moved anyway, and got a nicer apartment than the one they'd had in Miami. Maggie missed Florida and her friends every day. The school she went to in Chicago was much bigger than her high school in Miami. Tommy went to a different school, a few blocks from hers, and he didn't like it either.

Emma wanted to move to the suburbs, but Harry said he needed to live close to work. They had offered her a job in the hotel gift shop, and sometimes she snuck downstairs to visit Harry. They had been together for two years by then, and Maggie thought they seemed like strangers with each other. She tried to ask her mother about it sometimes, and Emma said she liked their life because it was safe. She said that was all she wanted now. She had put away all the pictures of Kevin, but Maggie had kept two of them in a drawer in her desk, where she could see them anytime, and she'd given Tommy one of their father in his flight uniform.

Harry looked like a fat little old man compared to their father. Kevin had been tall and lean, with a smile that wouldn't quit. Emma was thirty-two years old when he died, thirty-seven when she met Harry, and thirty-nine now. Maggie had friends with mothers that age and older, and they still seemed young and full of life. Emma looked like an old woman. Harry had just turned fifty and seemed even older. Maggie had thought her father was so glamorous, and her mother had been pretty when he was alive, but she wasn't anymore. She didn't seem to care, and Harry didn't either. He was a devoted husband, responsible, and accepted her as she was. She talked about going back to nursing sometimes but it had been too many years and the hours were too long, so she took menial jobs instead.

Maggie dreamed of going back to Florida when she finished high school. She missed the warm weather and the friends she'd made there. Moving to another town as a civilian wasn't like moving to another base in the Air Force. In the military there were always people to welcome you and make you feel at home. In civilian life, no one made it easier for you. You had to figure it out on your own, and meet new friends in a new school. And most of the girls were mean.

When Maggie turned seventeen after they moved to Chicago and started her senior year in high school, she ate lunch alone in the cafeteria every day. She hadn't made it into the clique of popular girls, and didn't want to. None of the boys noticed her. She didn't care about them either. Her grades were okay, but she didn't like her new school. She hardly knew her teachers. They'd never tried to get to know her. She was planning to go to a state college when she graduated, and didn't know what she wanted to study yet. Her mother had gotten her a summer job as a waitress at the hotel. She hated it, but she had no idea what else to do. She wasn't even sure that she wanted to go to college, but her mother said that her father would have expected it of her, so she felt she had no choice.

Maggie was leaving school one day, when someone flashed past her. She could feel the wind rush by her face. He would have knocked her down if he'd come any closer, but he was careful not to. She wasn't even sure who or what it was. When she turned around and looked, it was a boy on a skateboard, moving at full speed. He glanced back and waved at her. She hadn't seen a smile as dazzling as that since her father. He was tall like Kevin too, with sandy blond hair, and she thought he had blue eyes when he looked back at her. He was wearing a knit cap pulled down in the chilly autumn breeze. She was going to yell at him to watch out when he flew past her, but she didn't have time to. He was still smiling as he went around the corner and disappeared. He had frightened her for a minute, and then she went to meet Tommy at their bus stop to go home, and she forgot about the boy on the skateboard. She saw him again a few days later, on his way to school. He got off the board and carried it the last block to school, and came up alongside her.

"You're not supposed to skate on the sidewalk," she scolded him.

"I don't. I was just saying hi to you," he said with that enormous smile that started in his eyes and transformed his whole face. He had bright blue eyes and an aura of boyish innocence.

"You almost knocked me down." She frowned. She didn't know what else to say to him. She hadn't dated any boys yet. The girls in her class were much cooler than she was. She was an innocent compared to them. At seventeen she'd only kissed a boy once. He'd been drunk at a school dance and she'd run away from him. He scared her.

"I didn't almost knock you down," the boy said clearly. "I wouldn't do that. I've been watching you. Are you new at school?" He was curious about her and seemed more confident than she was. Her palms were sweating while she talked to him and tried to look indifferent.

"I was, last year. We moved here in April, from Miami."

He whistled. "Wow. Big change. The weather, if nothing else."

"The school too," she admitted. He had noticed her keeping to herself, away from the other girls. It was a big school, and not easy to make friends.

"Why Chicago?" he asked her.

"My stepfather got a job here, so we had to move."

"My parents are divorced too," he commiserated. "It sucks sometimes, doesn't it?"

"My father died eight years ago. My mom remarried when I was fifteen," she said in a soft voice.

"I'm sorry. That's tough. Cancer?" he asked cautiously.

"He was a test pilot in the Air Force," she said proudly. "And a fighter pilot in Vietnam. His plane malfunctioned, and it crashed. It was fun when he was alive. We moved around a lot. It's different in civilian life, and not so fun." She looked into his eyes as he held the door open for her and they walked into school together. He had said he was a senior too. There were a thousand kids in their class, which made it even harder to meet people, and she was shy. She'd gone to a lot of different schools until they moved to Miami, but she still hadn't gotten used to it. Being the new girl was hard. She thought civilian kids were much snootier than military kids, especially the girls. In the military, your status depended on your father's rank. Here, it was about a lot of other things: where you lived, what you wore, what kind of car your father drove, your parents' jobs. She didn't have any of the obvious status symbols the other girls did, which might have impressed them, so she didn't try.

"Your father sounds cool. I want to learn to hang glide when I finish school," he said with a grin.

"Do you want to be a pilot?" Her eyes lit up when she asked him. It was familiar ground for her. Finally.

"I want to be a lot of things. I want to race motorcycles. I've got a friend who lets me ride his on weekends."

"That's dangerous," she commented.

"So is everything worth doing. I want to jump out of an airplane and see what that feels like," he said, smiling at her, and then looked at her regretfully. "I have a class in five minutes. Econ. I suck at it."

"Me too," she admitted with a grin. "I like history, and Spanish."

"I hate school," he said, and lately she wondered if she did too. Her school in Miami had been smaller and easier to navigate, and she'd learned Spanish from her Hispanic classmates. No one spoke Spanish here. "Well, see ya," he said, and stopped at his locker to put his skateboard away. She walked past him to her locker at the far end of another hallway. It had been nice talking to him for a few minutes.

She didn't see him again for several days, and then he caught up to her leaving school on a Friday. She was hurrying, afraid to be late to meet Tommy at the bus stop.

"Want to see me race tomorrow?" he asked her. "My friend let me enter his motorcycle in a race. I just turned eighteen, so I have a license." She thought about it and decided she did want to see him race. It sounded exciting. She didn't know what her mother would say. She probably wouldn't like it, but Maggie wasn't going to ask her. Her mom didn't have to know everything she did. She'd have to find someone to leave Tommy with. She watched him for her mom on Saturdays, while her mother worked at the hotel gift shop. They had promoted her to manager.

"I babysit my brother. If I can find someone to keep him, I'll come. Where is it?" He told her. It was on an old track, a long bus ride from where she lived, but she was intrigued by him now. She realized she still didn't know his name.

"Bring your brother with you. How old is he?"

"He's twelve. He'd probably tell my mother, but he'd love to see the race too."

"Well, bring him if you want."

"Do you have brothers and sisters?"

He shook his head. "Nope. My parents got divorced when I was two. They fight whenever they see each other. I live with my mom. My father works on boats, all over the place. I don't see him much." She nodded. They each had their own heartbreaks to deal with. "What's your name?" he asked her then.

"Maggie Kelly."

"Paul Gilmore," he said, and they smiled at each other.

"I'll try to make it to your race," she promised, not sure if she could do it, and then ran to meet her brother before it got any later.

She was lucky. As soon as she met Tommy at the bus stop, he told her that he'd been invited to a friend's house the next day to hang out, stay for a barbecue, and then spend the night. He had made friends more easily than she had. But he was only twelve, and boys were less complicated than girls her age. Most of the girls had boyfriends, or they moved in a pack. She didn't have a pack mentality, didn't want to show off, and she didn't know how to play the games that attracted boys her age. Paul liked that about her. She seemed like a nice person, and she was easy to talk to. She was pretty too, in a totally natural way. She had shining dark hair, green eyes, and didn't wear makeup. She was tall and thin and had a good body. He had the feeling that she didn't know she was beautiful.

After she dropped Tommy off at his friend's the next day, she took the bus to where the track was. It was a bitter cold day. She had to walk the last few blocks and her face and hands were frozen when she arrived. There was a small crowd of mostly men sitting in bleachers, watching the track. She got there just in time to see Paul race. He came in third out of a dozen boys and men older than he was. They were riding mostly rebuilt motorcycles. The bike slid after he crossed the finish line, and he had a nasty gash on one arm and had grazed the side of his face. He was bleeding when she got to him, and she helped him clean the arm. He didn't seem to care that he was hurt. He was glowing with the excitement of having come in third. All the others in the race pounded him on the back and one of them handed him a beer. He didn't even feel the graze on his face in the emotion of the moment. He offered her a ride on the back of his motorbike to where he lived, which he said wasn't far away.

When they got there, she was shocked to see the seedy part of town he lived in, and the ramshackle house where he left his friend's motorbike in the garage. Then they walked back to his house, which was barely more than a cottage. It smelled of sour cooking and looked gray and dingy when they walked inside. He watched her face for her reaction, but she didn't seem to care. She was more interested in him than where he lived. She was the only girl he'd ever brought there.

"How does your face feel?" she asked him.

"Great!" He looked a mess and had dirt all over his jacket and had torn a sleeve when he cut his arm. "It's the best time I've had yet."

"Are you serious about racing motorcycles when you finish

school?" He nodded enthusiastically and had a light in his eyes that reminded her of how her father looked when he talked about flying planes.

"I am. I want to be the best at something when I'm older. Some kind of racing. I love motorcycles." She could see that he did. He poured her a soda from the nearly empty fridge, and they sat down on a sagging, beat-up couch and talked for a while, and then she said she had to go. She had a long ride home, and she wanted to be there when her mother came in from work. She didn't like to have to tell her where she'd been. "Do you want to go to the movies tomorrow?" he asked her, and she nodded with a slow, shy smile.

"Yes, I'd love to."

He walked her to the bus stop, and she thought about him all the way home, and that night. She didn't say anything to her mother. She met Paul at a movie complex downtown the next day. She was surprised to see that he was driving the motorcycle, and she rode on it with him after the movie, then let him take her to within a few blocks of her house. Her mother would have killed her if she had seen it. Motorcycles or anything high risk were strictly forbidden. Emma was afraid that she or Tommy would turn out to be like their father. She didn't even want Tommy to play sports, and all he wanted to do was play football when he got to high school in two years. He had the build for it, and his father's strength and agility.

Maggie liked being on the back of Paul's bike. It was exciting. She told him her mother would have a fit if she knew.

"She wants us to be safe, and not do anything dangerous. Ever since my dad died, she's been crazy on the subject."

"She's not going to like me then, is she?"

"Just don't bring the bike if you ever come to visit."

She didn't tell her mother about him until after Christmas, and then she mentioned him casually and said he was just a friend from school. She invited him to dinner and he came in jeans and an old leather jacket and sneakers. He was a good-looking boy, with his blond hair and blue eyes, and very polite, but Emma watched him with suspicion. There was a kind of self-confidence about him that was all too familiar to her, and that she never wanted to see again, certainly not around her children. He had a maturity which frightened her, and a self-assurance that came from the hard life he'd had. The apartment where Maggie lived was much nicer than the shabby cottage where he lived with windows that didn't close properly and the wind whistling through it.

"I'm going to have money someday," he told Maggie one day as they walked around the lake.

She smiled at what he said. "How are you going to do that? Rob a bank?"

"I don't know. But I know I will. And I'll buy my mom a decent house," he said, his eyes full of dreams, and the way he said it touched her.

"I don't know what I want to do when I grow up," she said. "My mom says all that matters is having a stable life and being safe. She says it all the time." Maggie was sick of hearing it.

"I don't care about that," Paul said. "I want to do something exciting. Climb mountains, race motorcycles, parachuting." His eyes were ablaze, as though he could see himself doing it.

"Roller coasters scare me. I'd rather die than jump out of a plane or go skydiving," Maggie said, making a face.

"I'd give anything to do that," he said.

Their romance lasted until spring. He had been Maggie's first serious crush, until her mother put her foot down. He said something once when he came to visit, about racing motorcycles after he graduated, and Emma came to her daughter's room afterwards with a doomsday expression.

"You're playing with fire," her mother said with steel in her eyes. "You don't know what you're doing. He loves danger, Maggie. He's a wild one. It's written all over him. Danger is like a drug for guys like him. He's like your father. And all that will ever do for you is break your heart. Sooner or later they die, and you're a widow. I want you to stop seeing him." It sounded like a death knell to Maggie. He was her only friend.

"I'm not marrying him, Mom. We're kids."

"He's not a kid. He's a young man, and he's dangerous. You could die with him if you're foolish enough to get on the back of his motorcycle. I'm not going through that again. We lost your dad. I'm not going to lose you or Tommy. Paul is a death wish waiting to happen. His eyes light up whenever he talks about racing."

"He's a boy. He'll outgrow it." Maggie was fighting for her right to see him. She didn't want to give him up.

"Boys like that stay boys forever. They don't outgrow it. They care more about risking their lives than he ever will about you.

The last time he was here he said he wanted to climb Everest one day. Maggie, stay away from him." Emma had tears in her eyes when she said it. Tommy overheard her from the next room and asked Maggie about it afterwards.

"Are you going to break up with him?"

"None of your business," she said, and from then on, Maggie stopped talking about him. They met in secret. She almost slept with him several times, but she was afraid to get pregnant, and she didn't feel ready. He tried to convince her otherwise, but she managed to hang on to her virginity until graduation. She had a lot to think about. She'd gotten into all the colleges she applied to, and had decided to go to Ohio State. Paul was taking a semester off before he thought about college. He was heading for Southern California to race, and see his father if he came into port while he was there. But his main goal was racing. He was leaving two weeks after graduation, while Maggie had another summer job at the hotel, until she left for Ohio in August.

Paul wanted to stay in California once he got there. He was going to go to city college somewhere eventually, wherever he was living. It was inevitable that their paths would go in different directions now. They knew it would happen. She was in love with him, but more than that, he had become her best friend. She could tell him anything. He knew everything about her, her hopes and fears, and how much she missed her father. It was like a tidal wave that washed over her sometimes. She didn't know how her mother could love Harry after someone like her father. But Emma was so frightened now, terrified of everything. Harry was exhausted when he came home at night, and she didn't want to go out anyway. It was hard to believe she was only forty. She seemed more like eighty to Maggie. She and Harry both did. All they ever did was watch TV and drink beer at night. They weren't drunks, but she could tell her mother was depressed and had been for years. Maggie wasn't even sure her mother loved Harry. He was the dullest man who had ever lived. But he was safe, which was all she wanted.

"When am I going to see you again?" Maggie asked Paul as the days slipped away. He was leaving soon. She was glad that she hadn't slept with him. She could see now that he couldn't be tamed. He would probably be a wild card all his life. Her mother might be right about that.

"I don't know, Mag," he said sadly. "I'm going to miss you." She believed he would, but not enough to stick around or come back. He was hungry for the world now, and all the risks he could take and wonders he would discover. None of that appealed to Maggie. She didn't have the thirst for risk that he did.

"Be careful," she said, and she almost let him talk her into having sex with him that night, but she didn't. She didn't want to lose her virginity to a boy she might never see again. She was more sensible than that.

Their last night together was bittersweet for both of them. She had told her mother she was staying with a friend, but they'd stayed at a motel, and each paid half of it. When the sun came up, Paul took off on his borrowed motorcycle. He turned to smile at her, with the sun shining golden on his fair hair, then he waved and disappeared around a corner. She walked home, feeling her heart ache, wondering where he would go now, what challenges he would conquer, what mountains he would climb.

He bought a motorcycle that day with money he had saved, and left for California. He'd called her the day before he took off, but he didn't come by to see her again. They both knew that their paths weren't likely to cross again. She knew she would never forget him. He would always be the first boy she'd ever loved.

Chapter 2

Ohio State was good for Maggie. The time she had spent with Paul during her senior year in high school had given her self-confidence and faith in herself. He had told her how smart she was, and how different from all the other girls. He made her feel special. At Ohio State, she majored in art history, and took classes in art and design. She took some business classes too. She thought they could be useful someday. Maggie was a beautiful, dark-haired girl with a good figure. She was a fine athlete, and loved going to football games with the boys she dated. One boy she went out with in her sophomore year wanted to join the Navy and become a SEAL. Her mother objected strenuously when Maggie told her about him. She swore he would be another danger addict who would break her heart, but Maggie lost her virginity to him anyway. Eventually they got tired of each other. She hadn't heard from Paul for a year by then. She'd had a couple of postcards from him at first. He had won a string of races in Southern California, and then headed to Mexico to race there. After that, he wrote and said he was thinking of going to City College in San Diego, but hadn't decided yet. The lure of all the things he wanted to do was greater than school. He wrote again that he was going mountain climbing in Argentina, and after that she got a postcard from him that said he was trekking in Nepal. He had told her he was taking any small jobs he could find, saving his money, and then taking off again as soon as he had enough to pay for the next step of his travels. He obviously hadn't gone to San Diego. She wondered if he'd ever settle down. She couldn't see it happening. The world was too big and too full of things that excited him. He had an unquenchable thirst for adventure, and she didn't. Not out of terror like her mother, but she just didn't want to roam all over the world looking for mountains to climb and challenges to conquer.

When she graduated, she went back to Chicago. Tommy was a senior then and, after graduation, nearly broke his mother's heart when he turned eighteen and joined the Navy. He said he could get a better education there. He wanted to be an aeronautics engineer eventually, and a Navy pilot. He did his officer training course the summer after graduation and owed the Navy three to five years after college. He did specialized training, flying fighter planes, and whenever Maggie saw him, he told her he was happy. He looked just like their father and loved flying just as much. His plan was to work for a company like Boeing when he mustered out after grad-uate school, and he would easily get a great job. His career path seemed like the right one for him.

Maggie had a good job then too, working in the finance office of a TV network. She made a respectable salary and had a small apartment in Chicago. Her mother and Harry had finally moved to the suburbs. Harry was sixty-one and planning to retire in four years, to play golf, watch TV, and drink beer with his wife, which was enough for both of them.

Maggie had discovered that she had a knack for finance, and had put her dreams of art and design aside. She wanted a solid job she could count on, and not have to take a risk by trying to develop a talent that might never pan out. She had learned from her mother the value of a sure thing, and how important being safe was. She set her sights higher than her mother had, but Emma had convinced her that safety was vital for a happy life.

When Tommy was twenty-three, flying for the Navy, they sent him to Iraq, which drove his mother into a constant state of anxiety. She quit her job at the hotel and sat glued to the TV every day, watching CNN, terrified of what she would see there. He had been in Iraq for four months, when her worst nightmare happened. His plane was shot down and exploded during the bombing of a convoy. There was no body to send home, and Emma looked like a zombie at the funeral. She never recovered. She clung to Harry as though she were drowning. He and Maggie got her up and down the aisle behind an empty casket, draped with a flag they folded and handed to her, just as they had the one on Kevin's casket nineteen years before.

Maggie was so worried about her mother that she quit her job, and spent three months taking care of her, but Emma was never the same after that. She looked dazed and distracted, and was frightened of everything. She cried when Harry left for work, and she rarely left the house. Her hands shook violently, and six months later, she was diagnosed with Parkinson's and dementia, but Maggie knew her mother was dying of a broken heart. Losing her son had killed her. She had lost two men to their love of flying planes, and their love of their country. And Maggie had lost a father and a brother. She was twenty-eight when Tommy died, and she felt different too. She understood better now what her mother had been trying to teach her, the importance of a stable, safe life. She never wanted to go through this again. She had nightmares every night, dreaming either of her father or her brother crashing in their planes.

She finally started looking for another job, when Harry hired a woman to take care of Emma in the daytime. She thought of looking for a job in a museum or an art gallery, but instead wound up working as a receptionist for an accounting firm. It wasn't an exciting job, but it was the best offer she had at the time, with a good company that had a fine reputation. The pay was fair and they let her do some minor bookkeeping. She told herself she'd find a better job later. She didn't intend to stay there forever, just for a while to get back in the workforce. It was a gentle way to start again after the trauma she'd been through. She liked the people when she interviewed. They all seemed straightforward and friendly and had integrity. It was privately owned by an older man, and run by his son, Brad Mackenzie, who was thirty-three years old and would inherit the business one day. They were considerate and kind.

They knew she'd lost her brother and had been nursing her mother, and were compassionate about it.

Two months after she started working there, Brad asked Maggie out, and she hesitated. She didn't think it was a good idea to date the boss's son. If it turned out badly she could get fired or have to quit. It seemed too risky, but he was so nice to her and so insistent that she finally succumbed, and they started dating. Even in her diminished state, her mother said Brad was perfect. The Mackenzies were a solid family and Brad was their only son. He had gone to Northwestern, played football in college, loved baseball, went to Stanford Business School for an MBA, then came home to run the family business and enjoyed it. He and his father got along well, and Brad told her repeatedly how much he had learned from his father. He was an all-around wholesome, decent guy.

A year after they started dating, he proposed, and they got engaged. She couldn't think of a single reason not to. He was the kind of man every parent wanted for their daughter. He wasn't exciting, but he was someone you could count on. And in a quiet, gentle way, she loved him. It wasn't a wild, passionate love, but she could see growing old with him. Their life wasn't thrilling, but it was predictable and solid, and having lost a father and a brother, with a mother slipping away quietly, he was a rock she could hang on to, which was important to her. She had no family left, except a mother with dementia.

She was twenty-nine when they married. They bought a home in Lake Forest, and she got pregnant almost immediately. Their son, Aden, was born when Maggie was thirty and Brad thirty-five, and they were the perfect suburban American family, the poster children for a happy life. Maggie's mother died shortly after Aden was born, which wasn't unexpected, and was a release from the grief that had drowned her. Maggie was glad she had at least seen the baby, although she thought he was Tommy, and didn't really understand by then. There was nothing left of the woman she had been before Kevin died, when Maggie was a child. The hard blows and the losses in her life had destroyed her.

Maggie had stopped working for Brad full-time when the baby was born, and helped him out two days a week when Aden started kindergarten. She liked working in the office with him. He had inherited the business by then, it was doing better than ever, and Brad was proud to own and run it.

He and Maggie were happy, more than she had ever expected to be. She had always thought she would marry a man like her father, handsome and rakish, daring and brave. Brad was an attractive man, but he had none of the wild impulses of her father or brother. He was what she had wanted, a man who was never going to surprise her or frighten her with a roller coaster ride through life. She didn't want that. She loved knowing that their life would continue on the same reliable path forever. She needed that now. Brad and Aden were all she had.

Her only worry was that Aden had the Kelly bloodline in his veins, and as much as she preached the same things that her mother had, about the value of stability and leading a safe life, risk-taking came naturally to him. He had climbed a tree at five and she had to call the fire department to get him down. He had gone too high on the jungle gym at school, fallen, and broken an arm. He was a ski racer at thirteen and fourteen, had a concussion at fifteen when he fell off a horse, and wanted to get right back on. She was constantly trying to tame him. He wanted to try every dangerous sport he could think of, and he loved going to skateboard parks with his board and learning terrifying tricks from the pros. It was hard to keep him down. He played lacrosse briefly in high school, which was a brutal sport, and rapidly switched to hockey, which was more so. He was a good athlete and had a natural aptitude for it. Maggie did everything she could to discourage him. Brad worried about it less than she did and said he was "just a boy," but she had seen firsthand what that could lead to, and she kept a tight leash on him, as best she could. She didn't want Aden to get hurt.

In his junior year in high school, he joined the ice hockey team and was the best player on the team. In his senior year, he was applying for hockey scholarships in college, which limited him to schools in the Northeast and Midwest.

"Can't he do something simple, like play tennis?" Maggie said to Brad unhappily. When she saw him do tricks on his skateboard, he reminded her of Paul Gilmore in high school. She hadn't heard from him in thirty years, but years before, she'd heard that he had become a legendary Formula One race car driver, which didn't surprise her. She was grateful that Aden didn't want to race cars or fly, but he wanted to do just about everything else. Maggie was constantly worried about him.

They had talked about having another child early in their marriage, but finally decided that one was enough. Aden seemed perfect to them. Maggie didn't want to take a chance that something might go wrong with a second one, while Brad wanted to be able to provide well for their son, give him a good education and a solid start in life. They didn't live lavishly, but they were comfortable. Maggie had always been sensible, and since she didn't bring in an income, she had never been extravagant. They had everything they wanted, and didn't need more than that. They could have afforded a bigger home, but liked the small, simple one they had. They always felt as though they had enough and weren't greedy for more, on any front. Brad had always been conservative and financially responsible.

Aden was going to fill out his college applications during the Christmas vacation, and Brad surprised Maggie two weeks before Christmas with the offer of a quick trip to New York. He was going to an accountants' convention for three days and invited her to come along. He didn't like to travel, but he went to a lot of conventions. The prospect of a little Christmas shopping in New York was hard to resist and Maggie loved going on trips with him. She didn't do it often, because she didn't like leaving Aden alone. But she called one of the mothers from the hockey team, and she was happy to have him stay with them. Maggie didn't like leaving him alone at home at seventeen. He was a good kid but not a saint, and the temptation of his parents being out of town might lead to mischief with his friends.

The day before the trip, Maggie told Brad everything was organized, and she loved the idea of staying at a hotel with him. Their life centered around their son and Brad's accounting firm, and they rarely took time off together. They had been promising themselves a romantic vacation somewhere when Aden left for college in the fall. Maybe Hawaii. Their life had turned out just the way Maggie had wanted it to. Her brother's death had affected her deeply. She was never as sure anymore that they were safe from the hand of fate. She was the antithesis of a risk-taker, and wanted to play it safe in all things, particularly when it involved their son. Maggie had seen what losing Tommy had done to her mother. It was even worse than losing her husband, which was bad enough. Harry was still alive at eighty, and had remarried a nice woman he knew from work. He visited Maggie from time to time, but had moved to Florida with his new wife when he retired, and he was slowing down. He rarely came to Chicago anymore, and he and Maggie had never been close. His marriage to her mother had been a sad chapter in his life, which she inevitably reminded him of.

It felt like a mini-honeymoon when Brad and Maggie left for the airport. Aden had been picked up by his car pool that morning. On the way to the airport, Brad and Maggie chatted about what they were going to do in New York. They were staying at a hotel they both liked and Brad had heard of a new restaurant he wanted to try.

There was a slight delay when they left O'Hare, but nothing major. The flight was more turbulent than usual, and it started to snow heavily half an hour out of New York. Brad glanced outside and wondered if they'd have trouble landing. He hoped they wouldn't be diverted to another airport, and as soon as he thought it, the captain came on and told them they'd been asked to stay in a holding pattern over LaGuardia for a short time. Twenty minutes later, they were told they'd be landing in Newark. The snowstorm had gotten much worse in the last half hour, and when they left the holding pattern and headed to New Jersey, they hit even worse turbulence. They dropped altitude, and the passengers could hear the landing gear come down. As soon as it did, the plane started to pitch and roll from side to side, and Maggie took Brad's hand and held it firmly. They could see that they were over the Hudson River by then, with the skyscrapers of New York on one side and New Jersey on the other, then the plane took a sharp nosedive downward. Maggie could see the river rushing toward them when she looked out the window. She glanced at Brad as the flight attendant made an announcement to take crash positions and told them what to do. The snow was swirling around them, they were going down fast, and passengers started to panic.

"Brad . . ." Maggie said, not wanting to say what she was thinking.

"It's going to be fine . . . it's just a snowstorm." He squeezed her hand and smiled at her as they took crash positions. Maggie was distantly aware of people screaming, and before she could say anything else to Brad, they hit the river with a bang, and a huge spray of water shot out around them, as the flight attendants shouted at them to follow the floor lighting to the exits. Brad put a life vest over Maggie's head and pulled her along. She didn't even have time to panic as passengers jumped down the slides,

half crying, some still screaming, a steady stream of humanity sliding out of the plane onto the inflated slides, which detached and
became rafts that were hit by waves of icy water, which soaked
them. They could see people sliding down the slides into the other
rafts. Boats converged on them and the plane sank lower as people
continued down the slides into the rafts bobbing on the water.
Maggie saw a woman slip overboard on one of the rafts and sink
under the waves, pulled down by her heavy winter clothes. Maggie had let go of Brad's hand and turned to him, but he wasn't
there. He was in the water, clinging desperately to the slippery
side of the raft with a frantic expression, as she looked at him and
saw him sink. She reached for him but couldn't grasp his hand as
the raft moved away from him. She screamed for someone to help
her, but he was pulled by the waves and the currents, and she
saw him start to disappear in the water. She screamed again and
pointed to him, as someone in another raft tried to grab him. But
as she watched, Brad disappeared and she couldn't see him anywhere, as passengers in both rafts stared at the dark, icy water in
horror. There was no sign of him.

All the passengers were out of the plane by then. Some were still
in the water. Two of the crew had jumped free of the plane just
before it went down, and boats were trying to reach them. Maggie
saw one woman in a uniform go down with the plane, and a man
was standing next to her. It was the captain who had stayed to see
everyone off, and then suddenly she couldn't see either of them, as

the plane slipped under the water, and sank to the bottom of the river. They had died heroes' deaths, while the helicopters hovered overhead dropping life preservers and ropes, and others shouted at the struggling passengers to grab them. Powerful searchlights swept the area as the desperate rescue missions continued. Maggie kept looking and hoping that Brad had been pulled into another raft, but she didn't see him. She sat shivering in shock in the life raft as the scene became a blur around her.

She felt powerful arms lift her up and put her in a harness. She had been soaked by the icy water, and felt herself suddenly flying over the river and pulled into a helicopter. Rescue workers instantly wrapped thermal blankets around her, and she managed to choke out the words, "My husband . . . he's still down there . . . you have to get him . . ." She tried to pull away from them to point to where she'd last seen him. It was a tangle of boats and rafts. The Coast Guard was on the scene by then with divers in the water. She was sure that they would find him.

Maggie was lying on the floor of the helicopter with rescue workers around her while they flew her to a hospital in New Jersey, along with other passengers lying beside her. One of them, an older man, was dead by the time they landed. Maggie had lost consciousness by then.

It was hours before the search ended. Seventy-two people had been rescued and survived, forty-nine had died, including the captain and two crew members, who had died bravely trying to save the passengers.

Aden was watching it all on TV at the friend's home where he was staying. He had no idea if his parents were alive, and he was sobbing as he watched the horror of it in the midst of the snow-storm, with rescue boats bobbing everywhere. They had recovered as many people as they could, but several had gone down in the icy waters.

Maggie called Aden three hours later, when she was conscious enough to do so, and she told him the terrible news that his father had died. They had recovered his body, but he had drowned. She had severe hypothermia herself, but they had managed to warm her and save her. Aden was still crying when she had to hang up, unable to speak any longer and shaking violently. She wanted to go home to him, but it was another three days before they would release her from the hospital and send her back to Chicago by air ambulance. Maggie was flown to a hospital in Chicago to be checked again before she was released. Aden had wanted to meet her there, but she knew it would be chaotic and traumatic for him, and she insisted that he wait for her at his friend's house.

When she came to pick Aden up, she looked like a ghost. It brought back all her worst memories of her own childhood, when her father had died, and later when her brother was killed in Iraq. And now it had happened again. A simple, easy trip to New York had turned into a nightmare. She and Aden went home to their silent house. They had already brought their Christmas tree home, but hadn't set it up yet, and left it tied up in the garage, along with the lights they didn't use that year. Maggie dragged the bare tree out to the trash on Christmas Day.

Brad's funeral was a week before Christmas. They buried him

with his parents in the family plot. Maggie's mother was buried nearby in the same cemetery, and the only family she and Aden had now was each other. He was inconsolable, and the entire community rallied around them, brought them food, and offered to do anything they could to help. Aden and Maggie ignored Christmas entirely, and kept to themselves, mourning Brad. She wished she had her mother to talk to, to teach her how to be a widow. She had no idea what to do next. She was consumed with guilt that she had survived and Brad hadn't. The questions went round and round in her head. Why had he fallen overboard? Why didn't someone pull him out of the water? Why was she still alive? She had no one to talk to about it, as she lay in bed thinking for hours every night and then wandering around the house. She hadn't even seen him slip out of the boat, and then suddenly he was in the water. She couldn't imagine her life, or Aden's, without him. Their life had seemed so perfect, and now everything was shattered. The airline had offered to arrange counseling for her, but she didn't feel ready for it yet.

Despite what they were living through, she helped Aden with his college applications during the Christmas vacation. They went for long walks together, and a few of Aden's closest friends came over. They sat quietly in his room, and he finally went out to dinner with them one night. Maggie sat alone in the house, and then looked into Brad's closets, as though she still expected him to come home and tell her it was all a mistake and he'd been taken to a different hospital. It just didn't seem possible that Brad had left her, as her father and brother had. They lived such a sane, careful life. They took no risks, did nothing dangerous. She had loved him for twenty years, and now he was gone.

The house felt like a tomb when Aden went back to school. Brad's office manager wanted to speak to Maggie, but she told him she just couldn't. She had no words for anyone. People were still leaving baskets of food on their doorstep, afraid to ring the doorbell. But she couldn't eat any of it. She couldn't imagine how their life would ever be normal again. She tried to be as functional as she could for Aden, but she felt like she was hanging by a thread.

Aden had somehow managed to get his college applications in on time, although he was telling her that he didn't care about college now. She had been nine when she lost her father and Aden was seventeen, still a boy in so many ways. How was she going to be both mother and father to him? Just living and breathing seemed nearly impossible. She was doing it but didn't know how.

She was sitting in their living room, staring into space in her nightgown, when one of the mothers from Aden's hockey team texted her that she was going to drop by, and then bravely rang her doorbell. Maggie didn't answer at first, and then finally opened it and stood there staring at her. There was no one in the world she wanted to speak to. She and Helen Watson weren't close, but Maggie had always liked her.

They stared at each other for a moment, and Helen spoke softly. "What can I do to help?"

"Nothing," Maggie said bleakly, understanding better now how disconnected her mother had been for years after Maggie's father died. "There's nothing anyone can do."

"Make beds? Do dishes? Cook dinner?" she offered, as Maggie smiled, stood back, and invited her in. She didn't really want to, but she didn't want to be rude. Helen was a nice woman.

"Everything's a mess. I haven't done laundry or made a bed since . . . it happened." She still couldn't say the words yet.

"I worked my way through college as a maid at the Four Seasons," Helen said with a smile. "You don't even have to tip me." Maggie laughed for the first time in weeks and the sound was unfamiliar to her. She felt as if she were lost in a strange new world, like Alice in Wonderland down the rabbit hole. It was suddenly a relief to have someone there with her. Maggie followed her around, feeling lost. Helen made her a cup of tea and handed it to her. She rinsed Aden's breakfast dishes in the sink and put them in the dishwasher and made order in the kitchen, while Maggie watched her. Helen opened the fridge, full of untouched casseroles and rotting fruit. She threw most of it away, then made cinnamon toast for Maggie, and went upstairs to make the beds, as Maggie trailed after her, looking embarrassed.

"I'm sorry, everything is such a mess . . . me mostly."

"It would be weird if you weren't," Helen said softly. "My identical twin sister died of meningitis when we were in college. I was a mess for months. You'll get through this, Maggie, I promise you. You just have to take it one day at a time, one hour at a time, or five minutes. I'm really sorry." Maggie nodded as tears filled her eyes.

"I can't stop thinking about it. If I survived, why couldn't he? He was bigger and stronger than I am, and such a good person."

"The mysteries of life," Helen said quietly. "Why did my sister get meningitis, and I didn't? Things just happen. And Aden will be okay too. You have each other." Maggie nodded, wanting to believe her, for Aden's sake if nothing else.

"My father died when I was nine, and my mother never really recovered. And then my brother died nineteen years later. I think that finished her." Helen nodded. By then, Helen had made the beds, picked up the towels and laundry, and headed downstairs, as Maggie went with her, seeming a little more alive. The house was already looking better.

"Why don't you put some clothes on and we'll go for a walk, just down the street, and then I'll pick up some groceries. You two can't live on week-old turkey casserole and shriveled lemons." She smiled and Maggie smiled back at her.

"I think Aden has been living on cornflakes and frozen pizza. I haven't been cooking." She went upstairs to dress then and came back ten minutes later in jeans and a sweatshirt, her hair properly brushed for the first time since the funeral. She suddenly realized how she must look to Aden, and felt guilty about that too. She didn't want to turn into her mother, shattered forever, broken by what had happened. She had to show him that they could survive, even without his father.

They went for a short walk, as Helen had suggested, and drove to the grocery store. Maggie didn't want to see anyone, but she didn't want to starve Aden. She herself had barely eaten since the plane crash and had lost weight. They filled the basket with simple, easy-to-prepare food, and went back to the house.

"Thank you, Helen. I just couldn't get it together."

"I know. That's why I came over." She was a pretty, petite blonde. She had three sons, Aden's teammate was the oldest, the youngest was six, and her husband was the head of an advertising agency in Chicago. They went to all their son's hockey games, just as she and Brad did. "Do you need me to make any calls for you?" she offered. Maggie shook her head.

"I haven't checked my messages in weeks. There's no one I want to talk to."

"It might be a good idea to check," she suggested gently.

When Maggie looked at her phone, she saw that she had thirty-nine messages. The thought of listening to them was exhausting. "I'll do it later," she said. Helen left shortly after, and Maggie sat down in the kitchen to listen to the messages. She had nine from Brad's office manager, Phil Abrams, at least a dozen from the parents of Aden's friends, four from their insurance company, and six from the airline. The others were from friends of Brad's and some people she didn't even remember, or want to talk to. She didn't want to talk to anyone, but she called Brad's office manager first, and apologized for not calling him back sooner. He had worked for the firm for twenty years, and she knew how much Brad respected him.

"Can I come to see you, Maggie?"

"I'm not seeing anyone just now," she said in a soft voice. He could hear how shattered she was.

"I don't want to intrude on you, but it's about the business." She realized then that she owed it to Brad to meet with Phil, no matter how hard it was for her. She couldn't just bury herself alive as her mother had done. And even her mother had gone out and worked. She hadn't hidden at home, she'd had her children to take care of. And Maggie had Aden, and Brad's business. She agreed to meet with Phil the next day, and said she'd come to the office. Then she asked him to call the insurance company for her.

"They don't want to talk to me. They need to speak to you. They've called here about fifteen times too. They're very eager to connect with you." She sighed and promised to call them. "The airline has been calling here too. I think you have to speak to them, Maggie. No matter how painful it is."

"I guess I do," she said, feeling exhausted at the prospect. She had forced Aden to go back to school, now she had to make the same effort herself, and face her responsibilities. "What do they want?"

"They didn't tell me. Their insurers probably want to speak to you, and their legal department. A lot of lives were lost in the crash. They're going to be dealing with lawsuits. Are you going to sue them, Maggie? That's probably what they want to know."

"Why would I? It won't bring Brad back," she said sadly.

"Call them, and see what they have to say," he prodded her, and she said she'd see him the next day at the office and hung up. She dreaded going and not finding Brad there. It would drive the reality home again. But she had to face it.

She had food in the oven when Aden came home that evening,

not a casserole and not frozen pizza. She'd made Aden's favorite meatloaf and he was startled when he saw it. She'd made mashed potatoes and string beans to go with it.

"You cooked?" He looked shocked.

"Jimmy Watson's mom came over today and got me up and running." He smiled and put his arms around her, then told her what she had planned to say to him.

"We're going to be okay, Mom. We're going to miss Dad like crazy." His eyes filled with tears. "But he'd want us to get through it. We have to do it for him."

"I know we will." She held him tightly, and a few minutes later, they sat down to dinner. She had set the table with place mats, nice plates and cutlery, and cloth napkins. Everything was going to be different from now on, and they both knew it. She had Aden to take care of, and he needed her. Brad was gone. She was a widow at forty-seven. She had no idea how they were going to survive this, but she was determined that they would. Helen Watson had gotten her back on her feet and moving forward. Maggie knew she'd never forget what Helen had done. She owed her a debt of gratitude forever.

After the meatloaf, they had ice cream and chocolate sauce for dessert, Aden's favorite. It had been Brad's too, but she couldn't let herself think about that. She had a son to get through his senior year of high school and into college, a business to make decisions about. And, like it or not, she had to call the insurance company and the airline. The rest could wait.

Chapter 3

The morning after Helen Watson had visited her, Maggie got up even before Aden was awake. She woke him herself, and he opened an eye, surprised to see her.

"What are you doing up?" he asked sleepily. For weeks, ever since Brad's death, she'd been up all night, haunting the house like a ghost, and fell asleep just before Aden woke up in the morning. He'd been making his own breakfast and leaving the house quietly, and his friends' moms had been driving him, since the students weren't allowed to drive and park their cars at school.

"I figured it was time to get back on breakfast duty." Ordinarily, she had made him a hearty breakfast every day. He had a long day of classes and hockey practice ahead of him. He was a tall, powerfully built boy, like Brad, and needed fuel to keep him going. He smiled as he got out of bed and headed for the shower, then she went downstairs to make him his favorite breakfast of bacon and eggs, sunny side up, and fresh-squeezed orange juice. She knew he'd gulp it down before he flew out the door. He was downstairs twenty minutes later, his hair still damp from the shower, and he was happy to see her. She looked tired, but as though she had drifted back to earth again, after nearly four weeks since his father's shocking death.

Aden was thinner and seemed suddenly older too. It was a hard way to grow up, and Buck Williams, his hockey coach, had been concerned about him, and had taken him under his wing. He knew from Aden that his mom had been close to nonfunctional since the crash, and was suffering from post-traumatic stress disorder herself, which wasn't surprising. Buck wanted to keep Aden on track, still coming to practice and focusing on school as best he could, despite the changes in his life. Buck hadn't asked but he wondered if they would have to sell their house and move, now that they were without Brad's earning power. Since Brad was the breadwinner, and he was gone now, anything was likely to happen, which could destabilize Aden's life even more than it just had been. Buck hoped Aden would be able to get a hockey scholarship, a full ride, so he could still go to college. He'd sent a note off to the athletic directors of all the schools Aden had applied to, asking them to consider his applications even more favorably, and Buck felt it was justified. Aden was an outstanding player, and might even have a shot at the NHL after college, if he wanted that. It wasn't what his parents had hoped for him, but maybe that would change now. Despite all of Brad's plans for him, Buck knew that the last thing Aden wanted was to become an accountant. Aden wanted to be a marine biologist, or a commercial fisherman in Alaska, or a test pilot like his grandfather, or preferably something outdoors and exciting. He had even thought about becoming a mountain-climbing guide or a ski instructor, none of which had pleased his parents. His future had been mapped out for him from the moment he was born. He was going to work with his father as an accountant in the family business his paternal grandfather had built forty years before. Brad had helped it grow into a sizable business, and it was thriving. They weren't rich, but they were solid and lived well, and everything they had and saved was focused on Aden, a burden he didn't enjoy.

Maggie dressed after Aden left the house. She wore a simple black pantsuit and tried to look businesslike. She had seen Brad's will, and knew that he had left her the business. She had no idea what to do with it, or how to run it. She liked working there two days a week, helping out, filing and putting things away, but she knew she didn't have the skills to take Brad's place. She wanted to keep it going until Aden grew up, and could start working there after college, but he was still years away from stepping into his father's shoes. She was counting on Phil Abrams to run it until Aden was ready. Probably after business school. She hoped he'd go to Stanford for that, like his father, or Harvard, but Aden wasn't the student Brad had been, at least not yet, and he was a much better athlete than his father.

The ride to Brad's office was short, and Maggie felt like she was on autopilot on the way there. She kept reminding herself that Brad wouldn't be there, so it wouldn't be a shock, but part of her kept expecting to see him in his office when she walked in. She looked pale and tense, bracing herself for disappointment when she arrived. Her dark hair was pulled back in a neat bun, her face was sheet-white, as it had been for a month, and she had worn no makeup. She had realized that there was no point, since she'd end up crying anyway. She cried almost constantly, although she was dry-eyed as Phil greeted her, and after hesitating for a moment, he walked her into his office. The door to Brad's had been closed for a month, ever since he'd left for New York.

Phil was older than Brad, and had worked for Brad's father. He'd been with the firm ever since he'd gotten his CPA. He was in his fifties and had put four kids through college working there. His son was a doctor, both his daughters were lawyers, and his young-est son was a CPA. Brad had viewed Phil almost as an older brother, and frequently sought his advice about practical matters, and run-ning the business after his own father died. They had stayed very much with his father's model, after modernizing it somewhat. They were highly respected in the community as a firm with integrity. Phil had thought of going out on his own early on, but once he had a family, he needed the stability that Mackenzie and Son offered.

"Would you like a cup of coffee?" Phil offered when she sat down.

"No, I'm fine," she said, but didn't look it. He noticed that her hands were shaking, and she kept glancing at the closed door to Brad's office, as though she expected it to open at any minute, and the large teddy bear frame of Brad to walk through it. Phil had felt that way at first too. He was a slight, gray-haired man, who looked older than his years. When Brad died, he felt as though he had lost a brother. He was still reeling from the shock himself. But he also knew that they had decisions to make.

"Are you doing okay, Maggie?" he asked, concerned about her. He hadn't seen her since the funeral, and she'd been through a lot herself, having been in the crash. She nodded. She didn't want to tell him about the headaches, the nightmares, or the sleepless nights. Her doctor had given her sleeping pills, but they left her groggy and hungover and even more depressed the next day, so she didn't want to take them.

"I'm okay," she said softly.

"I've been doing a lot of thinking, and it may be too early for you to talk about this, but sooner or later we need to think about the business. It's running smoothly now, and it could for a long time, but it's going to be years before Aden is ready to step into it, and Brad wasn't sure he'd ever want to. He's young, and he doesn't know what he wants to do yet. Brad wanted to be a professional baseball player as a boy, but he outgrew it," and Maggie knew that a broken elbow in his pitching arm had changed that, and he had settled into his father's business. "Whatever he decides, Aden won't be ready to take over for at least ten or twelve years. That's a long time, and Brad was part of the magic here. Clients need someone they can relate to, and I've always been more of a behind-the-scenes man."

"What are you saying, Phil?" Maggie looked worried and was

afraid he wanted to quit. She couldn't run the business without him, and she knew she couldn't do it herself. She wasn't an accountant and didn't have the skills. She was more of a girl Friday when she came in to help Brad out. She didn't deal with clients.

"I thought about it a lot, and I don't know how you'd feel about it, but I'd like to buy the business, or even enter into partnership with you. My son Bill is a CPA now, and he wants to come into the business with me. I'd already spoken to Brad about it, and he liked the idea. We need some young blood here, until Aden is ready. Clients like that too. But now we don't have Brad to run it. I'd have to step up to the plate on that. I will anyway. But I want to build something for my own family, a legacy we can count on and that I could leave them one day. If you're interested, I'd like to have the business appraised, figure out a fair price for it, and start paying you. I'd rather have full ownership, if I can afford it. I'd be willing to sell my house to do it, and put that money into what I could pay you. It would be worth it to me, Maggie. And, of course, I would preserve the name. Maybe we could call it Mackenzie, Abrams, and Sons. I think I might have just enough to pay you a decent price for it, if you could be patient, and let me pay you in regular installments over a year or two." She looked stunned. She wasn't sure how Brad would have felt about her selling the business, and Aden no longer having it as an option for a career later on. But she also wasn't at all sure that Aden would ever want to work there, and Phil was right, Aden was a dozen years away from stepping into his father's shoes, and maybe not even then. It was a long time to keep the business warm, and Phil would be retired by then, and couldn't help him. Phil was an honest man, who had loved Brad and genuinely cared about the business.

"I don't know," she said, looking confused. "I've never thought of it. What did Brad say when you talked to him about it?" He had never mentioned it to her, and she wished she could have his input.

"I talked to him about becoming a partner, and he wasn't opposed, as I mentioned. But things were working the way they were, so there was no rush. I never considered buying the business from him. This changes everything. We have to think about the future." She wanted to say "What future?" but she didn't. She had no future without her husband, and maybe the business didn't either. That hadn't occurred to her until now. She didn't have a clear idea of their financial situation, and didn't feel ready to yet. Phil had tried talking to her about it after the funeral, but she didn't want to hear it. She knew he was in the process of evaluating Brad's investments. Brad had been conservative and put back everything he earned into the business, then invested in the stock market himself.

"I have to think about it," she said, she felt like she was letting Brad down if she sold, especially so soon after his death, but he was a smart businessman, and she wondered what he would have advised her to do in their present circumstances.

"The firm will certainly be viable for a long time, but keeping it won't make much sense if Aden never comes to work here," Phil said. She agreed with that, but how could she ask her son to make a decision about his future at seventeen? That wasn't fair to him, to have to make such an important choice now, one that would impact them now and for a very long time.

"Do you think I need the money?" she asked him, and he shook his head and smiled at her.

"Brad wasn't a rich man by today's standards, but he was very comfortable, and wise about his investments. I've almost finished appraising the estate. We need it for probate anyway. I think he had close to a million dollars in his portfolio, including what he had saved." Maggie looked shocked. She hadn't expected that at all. Neither of them was extravagant, and he never talked to her about money. He just took care of everything and told her she didn't need to worry. She assumed he'd always be there to run it all. She didn't need to know about their finances while he was alive.

"A million?" She stared at Phil.

"Close enough."

"I thought maybe a couple of hundred thousand." And their house was worth something, though it was small. It wasn't in the most expensive neighborhood, but they were happy with it. "What do you think the business is worth?" It would be worth a little less now, without Brad, Phil knew, but he would build it up again, as he stepped up to the front lines and made it his.

"I'm not sure. A little more than that. Ballpark, maybe a million two, or three, somewhere around there. Brad had picked up some very substantial clients, and was still developing it. He was always trying to make the business grow. He taught me a lot. To be honest, that would be a big bite for me. But I've already talked to the bank, I could get a loan. And if we sell the house, I'd give all of that to you. Julie is willing to move into an apartment now that the kids are gone. It's a sacrifice we're both willing to make, and the house has appreciated more than we expected." They lived in a nicer house than she and Brad, and Phil had done a number of improvements on it himself over the years. They had added a pool when their kids were younger. "I think I can make it, Maggie. But it's up to you. If you don't want to sell to me, I understand. You don't need to sell. Brad had life insurance too, and they're anxious to speak to you." She suddenly felt sick. She didn't want to benefit financially from her husband dying. He had left her nearly a million in investments. He had left some of it to Aden, in trust for when he was older. But she had a roof over her head, and now Phil was offering her a lot of money for the business. With insurance money on top of it, she suddenly felt overwhelmed. She would have paid it all back just to have Brad alive again. She didn't want money instead of Brad, but at least it sounded as though she could pay for Aden's college education, even if he didn't get a hockey scholarship. That was something at least.

"There's no rush to decide," Phil reminded her. "I just wanted to put it out there, in case you do want to sell the business now or later, so you know how interested I am. And my son Bill would love it." She nodded, feeling dazed. If she sold it to him, she would wind up with somewhere around two million dollars. What would she do with that kind of money? She couldn't imagine.

He reminded her to call the insurance company when she left, and she drove home feeling distracted and separate from her body somehow. She should have been relieved about the money, but she wasn't. It just made her feel guiltier for surviving when Brad hadn't. And now she was making money from it.

She felt even worse after she called the insurance company. She had assumed that he had some ordinary policy, like fifty or a hundred thousand dollars she could put into Aden's college fund. College was expensive, and she and Brad had talked about that a lot. But Brad was a prudent, responsible man. He had been paying for years for a three-million-dollar life insurance policy, in case anything ever happened to him, so he would leave his family secure for life.

"Three *million*?" Her voice was a high pitched squeak when the agent she spoke to told her, almost as a routine matter, which he assumed she knew. She didn't. "Oh my God." It was getting worse. Not only was she profiting from his death, she was getting rich. In a single day, she had discovered that she had four million dollars now, with what Brad had left them and his life insurance policy. And if she sold the business to Phil, she'd have five million eventually. She hung up the phone, feeling frightened and confused, and half an hour later, she had a migraine headache and went to bed. She had taken a painkiller and was in a deep sleep when Aden came home. She woke up when he sat on her bed to check on her.

"Bad day, Mom?" he asked her gently. He could see that it had been. Most days were now. She was beginning to remind herself of her own mother and hated herself for it.

"Yes . . . no . . . I don't know. Kind of." Finding out they had four million dollars didn't really qualify as a bad day. Brad could have left her destitute or close to it, like her father had done, leaving only his military pension, but that wasn't her husband's style. But how she had gotten the money was devastating. She got up and went downstairs to start dinner. She brought up the business when Aden sat down at the table with her. She asked him about his career plans now, and felt foolish doing so. He was still the same seventeen-year-old high school kid he had been a month before, when his father was still alive. Nothing had changed, even if he seemed more grown up now. But his future was still a blank page to him, maybe even more so now without his father to guide him.

"Can you see yourself stepping into Dad's shoes at the office one day, when you're older?"

"Never," he said without hesitating. He could be more honest with her than he had been with his father, not wanting to hurt his feelings since Aden knew how hard his dad had worked to build something for them for the future. "I'd rather die than be an accountant like Dad. I don't know how he stood it. It's so boring, and I'm terrible with numbers." She knew that was true, but it could change if he tried to learn the business. Brad had actually enjoyed it. "I want to do something more exciting. I want to take flying lessons," he said, and Maggie felt her stomach turn over.

"Could we pick something a little more middle-of-the-road? Like a career where you don't risk your life every day? My father, my brother, and your father all died in accidents related to flying. How about something less dangerous than flying?" she reasoned with him.

"I'd rather be a plumber, or dig ditches, than be an accountant." He said it with fervor, and Maggie felt her heart sink, knowing Brad would have been disappointed too, although not surprised. He wasn't sure Aden would ever be cut out for the family business, although he'd hoped he'd grow into it one day. "Why?" She decided to tell him about Phil at least, not the insurance. She had decided not to tell him about that. He didn't need to know how much money they had now, not until he was older. She didn't intend to change anything about the way they lived. They had always been modest and discreet, and she wanted to keep it that way.

"I went to Dad's office today, to see Phil. He'd like to buy the business and run it with his son. He thinks it would be a long time before you go to work there, and he thinks it might make more sense if we sell it now."

"I will *never* work there," Aden said. "I told Dad that when we talked about it. I don't think he believed me, but I mean it. Maybe you should sell it, Mom." She nodded, not sure what to do. The idea was new to her and she needed to digest it. "Did Dad leave you enough to get by? Do we need to sell the house?" He had been worried about that since his father's death, but hadn't wanted to ask her and upset her. He wasn't sure what the situation would be with college if he didn't get a full ride.

"He left us enough," she answered softly. "We're fine. We don't have to sell the house, or the business if we don't want to. I don't want to do something your father would have hated, or that would have broken his heart. He loved the business and the fact that your grandfather started it. Maintaining it and making it grow was like a sacred mission to him."

"He was pretty practical, though, Mom. If you can't run it, and I don't want to, it doesn't make a lot of sense to keep it. Maybe you should sell it and invest the money. Maybe that's what Dad would have done," he said sensibly. It was the most adult conversation they'd ever had.

"I'll think about it," was all she said, and intended to.

The icing on the cake came after she called the airline two days later. She finally got up the guts to call them. She had been called by their legal department, the team assigned to settlements. They requested a meeting, and she wanted to put it off, but they said they needed information from her to better assess what had happened, so she felt obliged to meet with them the week after she'd gone to Brad's office.

They came to the house at ten o'clock in the morning the following week, and she met them in the living room. There were four of them. Three men and a woman, all lawyers. They told her very frankly that they had a clearer picture now of the circumstances of the crash. They had suggested to her that she have an attorney present, but she said she didn't need one. She didn't tell them, but she didn't intend to sue them. Whatever she or they did, it wouldn't bring Brad back, so she was going to listen but not file a claim against them, which was one of the things they wanted to know from her during the meeting.

They explained that on the night of the flight, whether or not it should take off had become debatable, given weather conditions in New York. It could have gone either way, and the snowstorm could have let up once they took off, or worsened, which was what had happened. But there was a strong suspicion before takeoff that LaGuardia would be closing shortly, and the deciding voices at the airline had decided to make a run for it. They had assumed they'd get to New York in time to be the last plane in. The pilot had thought he could make it safely, but they realized now, in hindsight, that they should have canceled the flight, to be completely safe. He was a seasoned pilot and had been part of the decision, and they trusted his experience and his judgment. The storm had gotten much worse after takeoff, and they had all been wrong. It was public knowledge and had been in the media, so they weren't sharing secrets with her. They expected numerous lawsuits for wrongful death to be filed, in which they would be accused of making irresponsible decisions. They were intending to shoulder the consequences.

At fifty-two, Brad had still been at the height of his earning power, and had a family to support. Maggie had been on the flight with him, and had suffered physical and mental consequences that might stay with her for years, or mark her forever. She had been clearly assessed with post-traumatic stress disorder when discharged from the hospital. The other passengers had suffered similarly, and many had died. It was not an event the airline was proud of, and they were prepared to accept full responsibility for it. They acknowledged that it wouldn't make up for her loss, or the loss of a father for a son, but they were prepared to compensate them in the only way they could. They offered her a ten-million-dollar settlement if she would sign a release. They were making similar offers to the other passengers, depending on the degree of damage they had suffered. One woman had lost her legs, a child, and her husband. They didn't tell Maggie they were offering her a hundred million. She hadn't accepted yet, and her attorney said she was still too traumatized to discuss it.

Maggie felt as if she were in shock again after they made the offer. They left her with the paperwork outlining their settlement package and the release she would have to sign, and advised her to seek the advice of a lawyer. They were kind and compassionate and very humble. Not knowing what to do, she called Phil after they left. He said he wasn't surprised, and thought it was the least they could do if the crash had been due to poor judgment on the part of the airline, which they readily admitted.

"You can probably get double that, if that's where they started," Phil said gently.

"I don't want double that!" Maggie said, horrified. "I don't even want ten million. I don't want to get rich because my husband died, Phil. You already told me we have more than enough from the insurance and Brad's savings."

"You have a right to that money, Maggie. You suffered a terrible loss and went through unspeakable trauma yourself. You should take it. It could make a big difference to Aden one day. I think Brad would want you to take it." She was shocked. It felt immoral to her, but pointing out that it might matter to Aden one day resonated with her. "You might even get more if you sue them, and they know that," he added, and she groaned.

"Is everything about money? I lost the husband I loved, and Aden lost his dad. Money doesn't make up for that."

"Aden could have seventy years ahead of him, and you could have fifty. He's a boy, and you're a young woman. Don't turn your nose up at that kind of money."

"I'm not. I just don't want blood money. It's bad enough that I survived and he didn't."

"It's damn lucky you did," he said, "for Aden's sake. Imagine if you had both died. What would happen to him now?" They had no other relatives and Aden would have been an orphan, on his own at seventeen. It suddenly made her realize even more acutely how important it was for her to make good decisions now, for her son's sake. She called Brad's lawyer after she talked to Phil, and sent him the paperwork the airline had left with her. She told him about Phil offering to buy the business too, and he thought it an excellent idea, particularly selling it to someone who knew it so well, had worked there for twenty years, and loved Brad deeply as an employee and friend.

It was a lot for her to think about.

The lawyer suggested that she turn down the settlement and ask them to double it. He thought she'd come out somewhere around fifteen million if she did, which he thought was fair, and he advised her again to sell the business to Phil, and said he thought Brad would approve.

In the end, she accepted the ten million the airline had offered her, which seemed like more than enough to her. More would have seemed obscene, for the price on her husband's head. She told Phil she would sell the business to him. They agreed on a million two, with two years to pay her in full.

When it was all over, she had fourteen million dollars, with a million more to come from Phil. He was elated about it. The airline's check arrived in the mail two days after she signed the release, and they thanked her for being so reasonable. Her lawyer had requested a confidentiality clause that they not disclose the amount of the settlement, or that there had even been one, so as not to make her or Aden targets for people with profiteering or criminal intentions, which she hadn't even thought of.

The insurance company's check took a little longer. Phil made his first payment right on time, as she would have expected him to. No matter how she looked at it, or hated the reasons for it, in a short span of time, she had become a rich woman. She didn't know what to do with the money, and hired the same investment advisor Brad had used. He had left her a legacy of stability, and a solid foundation he had built carefully. But she still had no idea what to do with it, or who she was without Brad. He had been her whole identity for nineteen years. Without him, she felt invisible, and lost. She had nightmares about the money sometimes and saw it dripping blood in her dreams, or floating in a pool of blood with the vision of Brad slipping under the surface.

She told Aden none of it, and she had accepted it all for him. She knew that if she safeguarded the money, as Brad would have done, and invested it well, Aden would be a wealthy man one day, but she had no intention of telling him or anyone else about it. In the meantime, overnight she was now a wealthy widow, which was the last thing she wanted to be. All she had wanted was to be Brad's wife, and a good wife and mother. Instead she now had money and had to live the rest of her life without him. At least they were safe and secure. It was his final gift to her. She would never have to worry about money or the future.

Little by little, the nightmares lessened, the headaches were less severe, and she was able to sleep at night again. She realized that despite how sad she was without Brad, security was a good thing. She was never going to do anything risky with her money or spend it lavishly. She would save all or most of it for Aden. It would be for him one day. It was the only way she could live with acquiring so much money as a result of Brad's death.

Chapter 4

At the end of March, Aden got his college acceptance letters. He was accepted at Dartmouth and Boston University, with a full scholarship to play on their hockey teams. Buck's recommendations had helped, but Aden had earned it. Maggie was even more worried now about his playing such a violent sport, but he had played all through high school, and it was what he wanted to do in college. It didn't reassure her that two days after he accepted Boston University, he got into a massive team fight on the ice, and got a cut over his eye that needed stitches and a dislocated jaw when the opposing team's goalie punched him. She gave him a sound lecture when she drove him home from the emergency room. Half the team was there, and Aden was proud of the scrap that they had gotten into. All of the boys were fined and would have to miss the next game. She was still annoyed at him when Buck came to check on him the next day. He was a big, burly man who had played professional hockey for two seasons in his youth, and had to give it up when he broke his ankle during a game.

"It's the nature of the game." He tried to soothe Maggie about the fight, which didn't reassure her. "The pros do it too."

"That's what I don't like about it. He could end up with a serious injury," she said as she led Buck into her kitchen after he visited Aden, who was watching TV from his bed. Aden didn't admit it to his mother, but he thought the fight had been fun, just like the pro players in the NHL, as Buck said. He felt like a man now, and Buck didn't disagree with him, although he didn't say it to Aden's mother. He knew she was always worried about Aden getting hurt. Other than that, Buck liked her. And she was a very pretty woman.

"He's a great player, Maggie. He's got what it takes for the NHL: incredible timing, speed, size. He's got all the right instincts. He could be a pro player one day, and a good one." She had higher hopes for him, and didn't want him playing violent sports. Brad hadn't wanted that for him either. "I'm going to miss him when he leaves for Boston. He's my star player," Buck said. She was more interested in his education than a future in the NHL.

"I'm going to miss him too," she said sadly. Buck had been very kind to him in the three months since Brad had died. He had mentored him all through high school, but had stepped it up when Brad died and tried to be almost a father figure to Aden. He had dropped in on him at home to check on him from time to time, which Maggie appreciated. There were no other adult men in his life now. "The house is going to be like a tomb without him," she admitted.

"What are you going to do?" he asked.

"I don't know. I haven't thought about it. Enjoy the next five months before he leaves, and then I have to find something to do. I can't sit around here all day." She had been thinking about it a lot, and hadn't come up with any ideas. She didn't even have her twice-a-week job at Brad's firm anymore. She didn't want to intrude on Phil, since he was buying the business, and he didn't really need her. She had just done it to be close to Brad, once Aden was in school.

Buck chatted about the subject awkwardly for a while, and then looked at her and spat it out. "I'd love to take you out to dinner sometime. You're a wonderful woman." He had been divorced for years and his kids were grown. His whole life was the school and the coaching he did. He was kind of gruff, a little rough around the edges, and he was great with the kids, but he held no appeal for her. She couldn't see herself with a high school hockey coach, going to games every weekend. She was ready for that time in her life to end. Brad had agreed to travel to please her, and they had both liked the theater and ballet. They went to Chicago for it. She wondered if this was what she had to look forward to now, dating the high school coach. The prospect didn't cheer her. She turned him down as gently as she could, and he looked disappointed when he left. She told him she wasn't dating and wouldn't be ready to for a long time.

Brad's lawyer tried the same thing when Maggie met with him. He'd been divorced twice and was something of a ladies' man, or thought he was. He was sixty years old, and Maggie was shocked when he asked her to dinner with a clear innuendo in his tone, and the look in his eyes made her skin crawl. She had always liked him until then, and decided to change lawyers as soon as possible. Helen recommended a friend, a younger woman at a local firm. Maggie met with her and hired her. She had no interest whatsoever in dating, and certainly not the dregs of what was available, either slimy men or lonely ones, who didn't measure up to Brad and didn't appeal to her.

She thanked Helen for the recommendation when they had lunch. They had gotten close since Brad's death. Her son had been accepted at Yale, and would be playing hockey too, but hadn't applied for a scholarship. They didn't qualify, and he wasn't a strong enough player to get one. Aden didn't need a scholarship now either, although he didn't know it. Phil Abrams and her lawyers were the only ones who did, and she intended to keep it that way. She had no desire to show off. On the contrary, she was extremely discreet. Aden's scholarship was based on his talent, and the schools he applied to offered it as a lure to get him to come to their institution and play on their team. It was not based on his parents' financial need or she would have felt obliged to decline it in their new circumstances, and would have had to explain it to Aden. She was glad she didn't have to.

"Wait till the married guys start hitting on you," Helen said with a wry smile, and Maggie groaned.

"Is that all that's left out there now for women like us? Married guys and creeps?" she asked with a look of disgust. "I don't want to date, and maybe I never will. But if I did, it's slim pickings. Who do people go out with at our age?"

"Old friends, people they went to school with, or met at work. Recently divorced guys, or younger ones. Or they meet online, but that always sounds scary to me," Helen said warily.

"I'd be terrified of meeting an axe murderer, or some guy fresh out of prison," Maggie said grimly.

"Or just a jerk, or a married guy lying about it. That's happened to a lot of women I know. But some of them do meet nice guys on the internet. I just wouldn't have the guts to try," Helen said. She was glad she was married, even if their marriage wasn't perfect.

"Neither would I," Maggie agreed about internet dating. But she was a long way from that. She still dreamed of Brad at night, and in her dreams he was alive. She still felt married to him when she was awake. She thought she always would. She couldn't imagine being in love with, or sleeping with, someone else.

"Have you thought any more about a job?" Helen asked her, and Maggie shook her head.

"I haven't worked full-time in eighteen years. I don't even know what I can do. And I don't want to do anything until Aden leaves for BU."

"Why don't you take a trip then?" She suggested it and then looked embarrassed. "If you can afford to, obviously." She was sure that Brad must have left them some kind of life insurance. He was a responsible guy, but she also knew Maggie was selling his business, and assumed she needed the money.

"I can afford a trip," Maggie said, "but traveling alone doesn't sound like much fun. And where would I go?"

"Why don't you make a list of all the places you've always wanted to go to and never have, and then pick? It could be really fun. Then start job hunting when you get back."

"Maybe," Maggie said, unconvinced. She loved traveling with Brad, but not alone.

She put the suggestion out of her mind. Three days later, she had bigger things to think about. Aden had gotten in serious trouble for the first time in his life. He and five of his friends had gotten drunk at a friend's house, broken into a skateboard park, and were doing tricks there with their skateboards. He had sprained his ankle badly but was otherwise unharmed. One of the other boys had broken a leg. The skateboard park had agreed not to press charges since the boys were first-time offenders from decent families, but they had been given a stern warning by the police. Maggie had to pick Aden up at juvenile hall, and then take him to the emergency room again. She gave him a serious talking-to when they got home.

"What's happening to you? You never acted like this before, when Dad was alive. Are you planning to turn into a juvenile delinquent now? Or get kicked out of school or off the hockey team?"

"I'm sorry, Mom." He looked remorseful and embarrassed. The beer had worn off by then. They weren't that drunk, just out to have fun. And he had a slight buzz on. "You wouldn't believe how high I got on the loops," he said, looking pleased with himself. "I want to go back there again sometime with my board!"

"So you can break an arm or a leg? I want to keep you alive and in one piece. You're all I have now," she said somberly. For an instant, he reminded her of her brother at his age, and Paul Gilmore with his skateboard before he graduated to motorcycles. She didn't want that for her son. But every now and then she could see that thrill seeking and danger were in his blood. It always had been, like with her father and brother. Brad didn't have that in him at all, which she had loved. "What's going to happen when you're in Boston and have no supervision? Are you going to go crazy, or behave? I don't want to lie in bed every night, terrified, waiting for the phone to ring and hear you're in trouble, or got hurt."

"You won't, I promise." But she wasn't sure she believed him. "Maybe I could be a race car driver one day," he said with a dreamy expression, and she groaned.

"You're not reassuring me, Aden. Maybe you should become a CPA like your dad. My mom was right about that. Thrill seekers and wild men always run into trouble. They either kill themselves or break everyone's heart or both. My father did, my brother was like that too, even though he died in the war, but he always loved speed and danger and anything high risk. I had a boyfriend like that in high school. My first love. He went off to race motorcycles and do all kinds of crazy stuff after high school. He's probably dead by now too. I don't want that happening to you. How would you feel if I became a trapeze artist in the circus, or a skydiver, or something where I could be killed?" He laughed at the image of his mother on the high wire.

"I'd think it was cool."

"Go to bed, before I lock you in your room and throw away the key," she said, only half joking. Sometimes he terrified her. More than ever now, without Brad's influence and fatherly control over him. And she also knew that if he had that kind of thirst for high-risk pursuits and danger, it would be hard to curb that as he got older and had more freedom. She hoped he stayed safe in Boston, and didn't go crazy without her watching over him.

Aden was relatively well behaved after that. Just the usual senioritis and hijinks before and after graduation. They cut some classes and sneaked some beer. He took a couple of driving trips with friends that summer, before they all left for college. He had a hot romance with a beautiful girl for the last month of summer, which kept him distracted. He spent most of his nights with her, and suddenly seemed very grown up to his mother. He was turning into a man right before her eyes. His summer romance left for UC Santa Cruz a week before he left for Boston, and he seemed to get over her quickly as he got ready to leave himself. It hadn't been a serious romance for either of them, just a fling. And the girl didn't try to continue it once she left, nor did Aden.

Maggie flew to Boston with him. It was the first time she had flown since the crash eight months before, and it was hard for her. After the crash, they had flown her back to Chicago, sedated, on a gurney in an air ambulance, and she hardly remembered it. But flying as a normal passenger with Aden was harder than she had feared it would be. She could hardly speak on the plane, she was so nervous, and Aden's attempts to distract her had been ineffective. She was sheet-white, and didn't speak until they got off in

Boston. Aden felt sorry for her, and wondered if she'd ever be able to fly easily again. But she had done it so she could help set him up in the dorm.

They had a trunk with them, and two duffel bags with all his hockey equipment. He was starting practice on the junior team in two days. He wouldn't be on the varsity team until junior year. And for either team, he had to maintain his grades. He would have to prove himself and earn his place there. He had already had several emails from the coach, who had a great reputation and was supposed to be tough. Buck had taken Aden out to dinner before he left, and told him to stay in touch when he was a big NHL star one day. Aden still wasn't sure he wanted to play pro hockey, but he was looking forward to playing in college, and doing a lot of other things. His life was unrolling in front of him like a red carpet. It made him miss his dad more than ever at times.

They got his dorm room set up in a day, with all his computer and stereo equipment, and a small fridge they rented. They bought a bike for him to use on campus. And he had snuck his skateboard into one of the duffel bags. Maggie found it and wasn't happy about it, but she let him keep it if he promised not to use it in traffic on the streets, and he agreed. Sometimes she wished that she'd had a daughter instead of a son. It would have been so much easier than all the different kinds of physical danger boys were attracted to, the men in her family anyway. But girls did other things to put themselves at risk, so maybe it was all the same in the end. She loved Aden with all her heart. It nearly killed her when it came time to say goodbye to him. She couldn't stop crying after she left, and she had to keep reminding herself, as Brad would have, that he was going to be okay. It was so hard doing this alone. And the return trip on the plane was even harder without him, but the flight was smooth, with no problems.

She felt drained and empty when she got back to Chicago, and had one of her worst nightmares that night, that Aden had drowned with Brad. She could see them both slipping under the water and couldn't reach them in time. She woke up sobbing, and sat up in bed for the rest of the night with the TV on, unable to get the image out of her mind.

She called Aden in the morning, when he was on his way to the store to buy his books. He sounded happy and busy and fine. He liked his roommates and rushed her off the phone. She sat down in her kitchen with a sigh. The house was as empty as she had feared it would be, without a sound, and nothing for her to do. Helen called her just as she was thinking of going back to bed, which she knew was a bad idea, but she couldn't help it. She felt as though she had lost everything now that Aden had flown the nest.

"So have you made your list?" Helen asked her.

"What list?" Maggie's mind was a blank.

"Of all the places you want to go that you've never been to. That was homework. Remember?"

"Yeah. I guess I forgot," Maggie said sheepishly with a grin. But she didn't want to go anywhere alone. "I can see them on the internet."

"You're not a shut-in, Maggie. You're a young widow with a kid in college. That means you have freedom. How about celebrating it?" It didn't feel like a celebration to her, and it made her miss Brad more. Aden leaving for college had brought the loss into even sharper focus. "I'm coming over," Helen said, and she was there twenty minutes later, as she had been off and on for the past eight months.

Helen had turned out to be incredibly loyal. Some of Maggie's other friends hadn't been. They acted nervous around her, as though losing her husband might be contagious, or she might try to hit on their husbands now, or her sadness and loss made them uncomfortable. Of all her friends, Helen had been the most present, and the most proactive. Every time Maggie started to sink, Helen dragged her up to the surface again, and got her going in the right direction. Except for this stupid idea about Maggie taking a trip by herself, which she didn't want to do. Helen insisted she'd have fun once she got to her various destinations. And she reminded Maggie that if she hated it, she could always come home. She wasn't going to the moon. She could cut it short if she really wanted to, but she should at least try to broaden her horizons again, and change scenery.

"I did it after my sister died, and it helped me," she said firmly.

"What do other widows do?" Maggie asked glumly, as they sat in her kitchen with her laptop on the table in front of her.

"They try internet dating, if they want to date. Change jobs, move houses, travel, take cruises, or get plastic surgery if they can afford to. You don't need it. You're gorgeous and don't look your age. You refuse to date and don't seem to want to sell your house, so that leaves travel. Turn on your computer." Maggie laughed. Helen had a piece of paper in front of her and a pen in her hand. She was taking the project seriously. Maggie wasn't. "Okay, so where haven't you been that you always thought would be cool?" Helen refused to be daunted, and stubbornly persisted.

"China," Maggie said off the top of her head.

"Really?" Helen was impressed. "Do you want to go there?"

"No, but I like reading about it. And Japan."

"Do you want to go there? Tokyo, Kyoto, the temples?"

"No, it's too far. I think I'd be scared. San Francisco," she said reasonably, and Helen wrote it down.

"Perfect. You get two points for that. What about L.A.?"

Maggie shook her head.

"No, we took Aden to Disneyland there. It would be too sad without Brad and Aden, and I didn't love L.A. But I've always wanted to see Big Sur, and the Napa Valley, and the Golden Gate." They were all locations in or close to San Francisco.

"Anyplace else in the U.S.?"

"No, we went to a lot of cities for Brad's conventions. I think we've hit all the high spots."

"Europe?" Helen asked her, enjoying the game. Maggie was starting to get into it too, in spite of herself, even if she never took a trip in the end. She didn't really intend to. She was humoring Helen.

"I've never been there," Maggie admitted, and Helen looked shocked.

"Never?"

"Never. Brad wasn't a big traveler unless he could justify it for business. He promised me that we'd travel after Aden left for college. I'm not sure he meant it, or would actually have done it."

"Okay, here we go. London?"

"Maybe. It looks cool and I speak the language," Maggie conceded. Helen wrote it down after San Francisco.

"Paris! You can't go to Europe and not go to Paris. It's fantastic." Helen wrote it down even before Maggie nodded. "Rome. Ohmygod. The food is so incredible and the country is so romantic. Florence is wonderful too, but less fun alone. And Venice is the most romantic city ever, maybe you should save that." She wanted to say for her next honeymoon, but didn't. "There it is. Four of the most fantastic cities in the world, if you eliminate Florence and Venice. You can do them in three or four weeks, and it will change your whole life and perspective. It beats the hell out of sitting around here watching TV, being bored, and feeling sorry for yourself. You said you can afford to travel. Call your travel agent."

"And I just go by myself?" Maggie was skeptical and nervous about it. And she didn't want to take all those flights alone.

"I'd go with you, but Jeff disintegrates if I leave him on his own with the kids for two days when I visit my mother in Detroit. Four weeks would probably kill him."

"It might kill me too," Maggie said, smiling.

"You can always come home," Helen reminded her again. "You'll never forget a trip like this, Maggie. And you have nothing else to do." Her son didn't need her anymore and there was no one else.

"I have to go to parents' weekend at BU in a few weeks." Maggie grabbed at a weak excuse.

"And after that, he won't be home till Thanksgiving. He won't even think about you by next month. You have plenty of time to travel. Grab it. Maggie, I swear to you, you won't regret it." Helen hoped she was right, if she decided to do it.

Maggie mulled it over all that night, and feeling utterly crazy, she called her travel agent the next morning and figured out what it would cost her. It was expensive, but she could afford it. And on the spur of the moment, she told her to set it up. San Francisco, from there directly to Rome, Paris, London, and then home. Four cities, four weeks, flying business class and staying at very good hotels, where she'd be safe. She had never done anything like it in her life, but she wondered if Helen was right and she should just do it. It was so out of character for her. But what else was she going to do between now and Thanksgiving except cry over Brad, miss Aden, and call him too often?

She was going to leave for San Francisco three days after parents' weekend in Boston. She'd miss Halloween, although she had no one to celebrate with. The travel agent told her that September and October were the best months to travel in Europe. It wasn't as crowded and the weather was still beautiful. She suggested a weekend in the South of France between Paris and London, but Maggie decided she could always add that once she was in Europe. The price for the whole trip was steep, but not totally insane, particularly given what she had now, and she was traveling in the best possible conditions, in total comfort at famous hotels that she had heard about and never dreamed she would actually see. She would never have gotten to Europe with Brad. It just wasn't on his radar, and he didn't have an explorer's nature. He thought a weekend in New York was as exotic as he wanted to get. It had taken ten years to get him to Miami, to show him where she had lived as a teenager, and he'd only gone because there was a convention there to justify it.

She called Helen when she hung up with the travel agent. "Okay, I did it. I leave from O'Hare to San Francisco. I'm going to rent a car and check out Big Sur and the Napa Valley. I'm staying at the Fairmont on Nob Hill, and I'm flying from there to Rome five days later, staying at the Hassler above the Spanish Steps. A week there, then to Paris, staying at the Ritz, and then Claridge's in London and home."

"I'm proud of you," Helen said and meant it. "I couldn't afford all that when Jenna died, but I got a Eurail pass and traveled all over Europe for a summer. I felt alive again after that, went back to school and finished, and then I met Jeff in my first job after I graduated. I don't think I'd have been the same person if I hadn't taken that trip. I didn't think I had permission to live or have fun after she died. And then I realized that she would have wanted me to. She didn't want me to mourn her forever. And she would have done it if I died."

"Brad would never have gone on a trip like this if I died," Maggie said. "He'd have hated it."

"No, but he might have gone to Hawaii, or Wyoming or Montana, or Mexico for a vacation."

"He might have," Maggie conceded.

"You have to give yourself permission to go on living. This is a terrific way to do it. And maybe you'll meet the man of your dreams," she teased her.

"Brad was the man of my dreams," she said sadly.

"I know he was," Helen said, instantly respectful. "But you can't bury yourself with him. That's not good for you or Aden. Your doing something like this trip gives him permission to still have fun too."

Maggie smiled. "I think Aden Mackenzie needs a little *less* permission to have fun," she said ruefully, and they both laughed.

For the next three weeks, Maggie read up on the cities she was going to, and still couldn't believe she was doing it. She told Aden, and he was shocked but supportive.

"That's fantastic, Mom. I want to go to Europe with you one day. Some of the guys from home are talking about going next summer. I want to go with them. Maybe we can meet up." Suddenly she was becoming a world traveler, and Aden even wanted to join her on a future trip. Maybe she'd go to Venice next summer, and Spain, or Scandinavia. The whole world seemed to be opening up in front of her. And she was seeing it all in the safest, most comfortable way. Brad had made that possible with the money he'd left her. She didn't like to think about the settlement money and the reason for it. She considered it untouchable and wanted to leave it to Aden one day, and she certainly didn't need it. She had more than enough from their savings, his insurance, and what Phil Abrams was paying her regularly.

She packed for Europe before she left for parents' weekend in Boston. The flight was a little easier this time, since she had already flown twice, and had never been a nervous flyer before. It was good practice before the flights she'd be taking in Europe, which had concerned her. She had a wonderful time with Aden and his new friends. She and Aden took several of them out to dinner, and then she flew home to Lake Forest, spent two nights at home, and left for San Francisco. She had bought some new clothes for the trip, nothing fancy, just some comfortable sports clothes to travel in, some pretty sweaters, and new jeans. Everything had been set up. Her reservations had been confirmed.

She drank a glass of champagne to steady her nerves on the flight to San Francisco. She had called Helen the night before she left, promised to text her along the way, and thanked her for giving her the courage to do it. Encouraging her to go was the best gift anyone had given her since Brad died.

As the plane touched down in San Francisco on a glorious fall day, Maggie was smiling. She got off with a bright red tote bag she'd just bought, and headed for the first stop on her big adventure. She knew as she headed toward the city in the car she had rented at the airport, that her life was about to change forever. In a good way this time. She was ready for it, and she suddenly felt that Brad would have been proud of her, it was almost as though she had his blessing and permission to do it. Helen was right.

Chapter 5

Maggie followed the directions from the GPS in her rented car on her way into the city from the airport. It seemed like an easy city to navigate. She got to the elegant Fairmont hotel on the top of Nob Hill half an hour after she left the airport. The hotel was huge, with several restaurants, many shops, gigantic chandeliers, and a grand lobby. It was a throwback to another era and Maggie loved it. Across the street was the famous Pacific-Union Club, which had been one of the most magnificent old family homes in San Francisco. Across Huntington Park was the splendor of Grace Cathedral. And all around them in the distance was the San Francisco Bay, dotted with sailboats.

Maggie had reserved a junior suite with a sitting area, and beyond her windows she could see both the Golden Gate Bridge and the new Bay Bridge, with Alcatraz in the vista between them. She stood and stared at it all for a moment, after the porter set her bags down. She stayed in the room just long enough to put on jeans and running shoes, freshen up, have a cup of tea, and then set out on foot to discover the city. So far, it was everything she had thought it would be: picturesque, architecturally lovely, and geographically beautiful. It had a charming feel to it and was a small city.

She walked down Nob Hill to Chinatown, wandered past all the colorful shops, and then turned south toward Union Square, where all the big fancy stores were. Then, for the fun of it, she took a cable car up the hill, back to the hotel. She called Helen from the cable car.

"Okay, I'm here," she said, and Helen could hear the clanking of the bell and the traffic around them. "I'm doing it." Maggie loved it, and she didn't even mind exploring alone so far.

"I'm proud of you," Helen told her before they hung up. Maggie got her car out and drove around the city after that. To Coit Tower on the top of Telegraph Hill, North Beach, the old Italian section, Ghirardelli Square, and Fisherman's Wharf, where all the tourist shops were. Then she drove to Pacific Heights to admire all the elegant houses in the best residential part of town, on the strip of Upper Broadway called "The Gold Coast." She parked her car in the Marina after that, and walked through the Presidio, the old military base, as far as the Golden Gate Bridge, which looked majestic glinting in the sunlight. It was a beautiful warm day, so she went back to get her car and then drove across the bridge, and up on top of the Marin Headlands for a spectacular view of the city. She texted Helen pictures of it and the Golden Gate, and once in

Marin, she drove along a winding road to a beach she had read about, which was a three-mile expanse of white sand with hardly any people on it. Just a few dogs and their owners, walking at the edge of the surf. Maggie sat down on the sand to admire the view. She put sand dollars and shells she had picked up in a small pouch in her purse. As she sat there, she thought of Brad and how he would have loved it. But she loved it too, and she realized that she didn't feel lonely sitting there. It empowered her and made her come alive. For once, she didn't feel guilty about it, just grateful to be there. It was the first time she had felt that way since Brad died. A big dog came bounding up to her at one point, a friendly chocolate Lab. He sat next to her, as though to keep her company, and then he loped off.

She stayed on the beach until almost sunset, then drove back along the winding road she had arrived on. She got to the hotel at seven o'clock. She had thought about going out to dinner, but she had done so much that day, and walked so far, that she decided to stay in and order room service instead. When she took her jeans off, she smiled. She had brought a little mountain of sand home in her running shoes. She carefully put the shells she'd collected in a pocket of her suitcase. They were the first souvenir of her trip.

She had a hamburger and watched one of her favorite movies on TV and went to bed early. She spent the next day exploring the Napa Valley. The vineyards looked like photographs she'd seen of Italy and France. There were beautiful wineries, and lovely homes, and some Victorian houses near the vineyards. There were lots of people on bicycles, but fewer tourists at that time of year, and the weather was warm, noticeably hotter than in the city. It was every bit as pretty as she had hoped it would be. When she went back to the city that night, she stopped at a Japanese restaurant she'd read about and had sushi. She felt as though she was having the full San Francisco experience, and wished that Aden was with her. She called him at school and told him all about it.

"You sound great, Mom," he said to her, and she felt great, totally alive. "What's next?"

"I'm driving down to Carmel and Big Sur tomorrow." She wanted to see the sea lions, the famous aquarium in Monterey, and the rugged coastline of Big Sur. She was staying at a place called the Post Ranch for a night, and then returning to San Francisco to see whatever she had missed.

Aden was already busy practicing with the hockey team and said he loved it. They both sounded happy when they hung up, each of them enjoying new adventures.

After she called him, a couple leaned over from the next table, smiling at her.

"A freshman son?" the woman asked her, and Maggie nodded. "It nearly killed me when our son left. He's a junior now, and we take trips we never took before. We love it." They said they were from Dallas and they chatted for half an hour before Maggie paid and left to go back to the hotel. It made her feel less solitary just talking to them.

By the end of the week, Maggie had seen everything she wanted to see. She had chatted with people in several places, from all over the United States. She felt brave and independent after her first stop. The timing was perfect. She had been there for five days. On the sixth, she caught her flight to Rome in the afternoon, for the next leg of the trip.

On the plane, she sat next to an Italian professor, who told her fascinating stories about the city she was about to discover for the first time. It distracted her from any nervousness she had about the flight. He was somewhere in his seventies and very charming. He said he had a daughter about her age, but she had the distinct impression that he was flirting with her, which seemed flattering and funny and very Italian.

She slept for half of the trip, after a delicious meal in business class, and arrived refreshed in Rome. The professor wished her a good trip. He said his wife was picking him up. He had failed to mention her before.

The hotel had sent a car and driver to pick her up, and the driver explained all the historical sights to her as they drove into the city. She couldn't wait to get started. It was four in the morning in Lake Forest, or she would have called Helen to tell her about it. She texted her instead, along with a photograph of the Colosseum and the entrance to the hotel. There were liveried porters and doormen. One of the managers from the front desk showed her to her small elegant room, with a balcony and a view of Rome that was breathtaking. She stood staring at it for a minute after he left, and felt as though she had been born again. It was one of the most exciting moments of her life. She was seeing history and modern-day beauty combined, with St. Peter's and the Vatican in the distance, the Spanish Steps beneath her, and young people sitting around the fountain below, some of them kissing. She wanted to toss a coin in the fountain later for good luck, and was told she had to throw a coin in the Fontana di Trevi while she was there, to assure that she'd come back to Rome.

Her driver was waiting for her when she emerged from the hotel an hour later wearing a wide black cotton peasant skirt with sandals, with her dark hair loose on her shoulders.

"You look Italian," the driver, Luigi, said, smiling at her.

"Irish," she corrected him. She got into the Mercedes the hotel had provided, and he drove her to famous churches she had read about and seen in photographs, and tiny churches tucked into little squares and backstreets. They stopped so she could eat a gelato. She wanted to drink Rome in and see everything. Being there was magical. She would have loved to share it with someone, but she wasn't lonely, and for now texting Helen was enough. Everywhere she went, people were friendly and chatted with her, or said hello. She talked to a Canadian couple, a very lively older Swedish woman, and a very attractive Italian man tried to pick her up at a café. She didn't let him pursue it, but she liked knowing that she could have. The men in Rome looked at her in a way that no man had in years. It made her feel young again, and attractive, and put a spring in her step when she noticed it.

She walked for hours every day and used the car when she needed it. The driver took her to small, out-of-the-way trattorias and restaurants with outdoor seating, where she ate delicious meals and enjoyed watching the people at nearby tables. There was so much to see and do, she didn't even mind being alone. At night, which was afternoon in Chicago, she called Helen and told her all about it.

"I think Rome is my favorite city in the world," Maggie told her breathlessly. "If I were younger, I would want to live here." But it was too late for that. She had a life and a son, except that her life as she knew it had ended nine months before, and her son was going to be living in Boston for four years. Still, she couldn't imagine just moving to Europe. But visiting was even more exciting than she had hoped.

"You haven't even seen Paris yet. You'll never want to come back after that, although Italian men are much bolder." Maggie couldn't imagine a city she'd love more than Rome. The music, the street life, the food, the people, even the other tourists she met were interesting and fun to talk to. The city was just chaotic enough to be charming without being overwhelming. Even when she got lost when she went out on walks, she always managed to find her way to the Piazza di Spagna, and the hotel above it. She felt totally at home, and much better at fending for herself in a foreign city than she ever thought she would be. It was an amazing confidence booster. She would never have experienced it in the same way if Brad had been with her. Being on her own forced her to reach out, connect with her surroundings and other people, and she blossomed.

"Why have I never been here before?" she said to Helen one night from her balcony, admiring the night sky of Rome. The world seemed so much bigger from here than in the life she had been living for decades with Brad in Lake Forest. He had kept their life small and safe and controlled, she had never realized before how much more exciting life was in a broader world, and how much she would love it.

"You've never been there because your husband was American, and he didn't like to travel, except to accountants' conventions. Maybe you'll find a European next time," Helen said gently. She had always found Brad very dull, but would never have said that to Maggie.

"There won't be a next time," Maggie said, sounding certain of it. "I've had my life with Brad. I can't imagine life with someone else. But I have to admit, I wouldn't mind living here for a few months or a year." She hadn't changed her lifestyle at all since the fortune that had befallen her when Brad died. She felt too guilty to spend it, but for the first time she realized the opportunities she had now that she'd never had before, and this was one of them. She loved the idea of traveling more.

"If you can afford to do that, you should," Helen encouraged her. "If something happened to Jeff, and the kids were grown up, I think I'd live in Paris for a year. That's my favorite city." Maggie couldn't imagine any place that she'd love more than Rome. She was sorry she and Brad had never gone there in his lifetime. Even an inveterate non-traveler would fall in love with it. She thought it was the most romantic city on earth, and she didn't even mind being there alone.

She was genuinely sad when she left Rome the next day to fly to Paris. Her driver, Luigi, hugged her, and told her to come back again. He had seen to it that on one of their drives she had thrown a coin into the Fontana di Trevi, which he assured her was guaranteed to bring her back to Rome.

The flight to Paris took less than two hours. Things seemed to be moving more quickly in the Paris airport, and didn't have the leisurely feeling of Rome, although the airport in Rome had been chaotic. Paris seemed more organized and a little less welcoming.

The hotel had arranged a car and driver for her there too. The driver's name was Florent, and he sped her toward the city on the highway, which looked no different than an American highway, until they reached the city. As soon as they got there, it took her breath away. The sight of the Champs-Élysées stretching toward the grandeur of the Arc de Triomphe, with a huge French flag fluttering under the arch, the wide tree-lined street, and the splendor of the Place de la Concorde with its fountains and sculptures. She had seen countless movies filmed there, but nothing brought it home like being there. She could see the beautiful bridges, Napoleon's tomb in the Invalides with its gold dome on the other side, on the Left Bank. After crossing the gilded Alexander III Bridge back to the Right Bank, they entered the Place Vendôme with its Napoleonic battle monument in the center, elegant jewelry shops all around the square, and the grandeur of the Hôtel Ritz, with a fleet of doormen and a wide red carpet leading up the front steps as though to welcome her. She had chosen the most elegant possible way to see Paris and get to know the city. Paris had an entirely different flavor from Rome, which was a venerable ancient city, filled with beautiful old monuments, and young people who looked happy and sexy. There was a spirit of romance there, which was contagious. Paris was sheer beauty at its most dazzling. Everywhere Maggie looked there was something beautiful to see. It was a whole different experience, and she could see instantly why Helen loved it. Who wouldn't?

Her room at the Ritz was bigger and even more elegant than her room had been at the Hassler, since the Ritz had been recently renovated. It was filled with antiques and beautiful fabrics. It was done in blue silk, while at the Hassler it was yellow satin. She realized that after this experience it was going to be hard to go home and live a normal, ordinary life in a small house in a suburb of Chicago. Here she was surrounded by beauty and history and exquisite monuments and buildings everywhere.

She went to the Louvre that afternoon, and strolled through the Tuileries Garden. The driver took her past all the fancy shops on the Faubourg Saint-Honoré, like the Via Condotti in Rome. She hadn't done much shopping so far. She was too excited by the city itself to do so. There was nothing she wanted or needed except to be here and soak up the elegance and atmosphere, which were the essence of the city.

She loved walking along the Seine, the river that ran through Paris, and she stopped sometimes on one of the bridges, just looking into the water and thinking about Brad, and her mother, and how difficult her life must have been after losing her husband. She hadn't had the luxury of a trip to Europe in opulent circumstances to help her recover. She had had to move from city to city and job to job to support her family. It had taken her five years to meet Harry, who gave her some degree of security, but until then everything had been a struggle, and even sometimes after that. She didn't want to burden Harry with another man's children, so she had done her best to support Maggie and Tommy herself with the jobs she had. She wondered if her mother would have been happier if she'd gone back to nursing, but she had never wanted to go back to school, so she took whatever meaningless jobs she could get that she never really liked. Her life had been far from easy and rarely satisfying on any level. Maggie's father had left them unprepared and ill equipped to survive life without him. And her mother had never been happy again, even with Harry.

Brad had been just the opposite from her father, and had protected Maggie and Aden from anything that might happen if he died. His insurance policy had cost him a fortune in his lifetime, sometimes even more than he could afford, Maggie realized. But it provided her with a lifestyle that she had never dreamed of, like this trip, which was possible for her now. Even after his death he had taken care of her handsomely, which was so typical of Brad. And Aden would have a solid foundation under him, and a great education, without their ever touching the money from the airline. Brad had already given them everything they needed. The airline money was just an unimaginable bonus, like winning the lottery, and she wanted that money to go to Aden one day for having lost his father so young.

Maggie felt incredibly blessed and lucky as she explored the Left and Right Banks, walked past every monument, went to museums, hunted for famous statues in tiny parks, and fell in love with the Rodin Museum. She took herself to tea at the Plaza Athénée and La Durée, had lunch at the famous Café de Flore and the Deux Magots, dug around in antique shops, and admired the spectacular flower arrangements by Jeff Latham in the lobby of the Hotel George V. She bought flowers from a street vendor and asked a maid at the Ritz to put them in a vase. It was another incredibly romantic city, and she wished she had seen it with Brad, but she was so happy there and so busy once again that she didn't mind being alone, and reminded herself that this was now her life, having to experience everything on her own. She was slowly making her peace with it, adjusting to her solitude and new circumstances. She couldn't imagine sharing her life again with someone else. It felt like her destiny now to be on her own. She chatted easily with people in museums and bistros, some of them Americans, others from all over Europe. Every day was an adventure and every encounter interesting.

She could easily see why Helen said she wanted to live there for a year. Maggie couldn't imagine being lonely there. The underlying feeling was one of contentment and peace, and a rich abundance of beauty all around her. When she woke early in the morning and looked out over the Place Vendôme, the light was a soft luminous pearl-gray washing over the rooftops until the sun broke through the clouds a little later and bathed all in sunlight with blue skies. It stayed light very late at night, until ten o'clock. She could see why it was called the City of Light. And she loved watching the Eiffel Tower sparkling in the night sky on the hour.

She was picking up her key at the desk one afternoon, when she saw a brochure for a very grand-looking hotel in Monaco. It reminded her of her travel agent's suggestion to visit the South of France if she had time. Monaco was a tiny principality, nestled along the French coastline. It was where Grace Kelly had married a storybook prince in the 1950s and become Princess Grace of Monaco. Maggie looked at the brochure for a minute and inquired about it at the desk.

"Is it complicated to get there?" She wasn't sure where it was.

"Oh no, madame, it's a short hour's flight. It's quite close. Directly south, on the Riviera." He mentioned Saint-Tropez too, which was more of a beach town, and very fashionable. According to the concierge, Monte Carlo was a tiny city, with a port full of yachts and a very international group of visitors, great restaurants, and an elegant casino where people gambled and played blackjack and roulette. It sounded like fun to Maggie, and a little bit old-fashioned, which appealed to her. She was going to London, but the concierge said she could easily fly from Nice to London. He said the weather in the South was excellent at this time of year, and still very warm. She could lie by the pool at her hotel after she saw the sights. It would be a pleasant interlude between Paris and the hubbub of London. She was in no rush to get back to the States. She had adjusted to the more leisurely pace of Europe, where quality of life was all-important. She could feel her own rhythm slow as she explored first Rome and then Paris. Monte Carlo seemed like an excellent stop on the way to London. She had seen everything she wanted to in Paris, although she hated to leave, just as she had been sad to leave Rome. But she was sure she would come back again, and maybe see Venice next time, and other European cities, like Barcelona or Madrid. Her trip had been perfect so far, at just the right speed, but there was so much more to see that she hadn't seen on this trip. She was feeling adventuresome, which was new for her. She had met several other widows, some of them traveling together. They were older than she was, but there was a kind of unspoken understanding between them, like a secret club.

On the spur of the moment, she asked the concierge to book her a room at the Hermitage in Monte Carlo for the weekend. She could leave for London on Monday, and was planning to spend a week there before she went home.

He called her in her room a few minutes later and told her it was all confirmed. She was on a ten o'clock flight the next morning, would fly into Nice, and be at the Hermitage by noon, which would give her a whole day to explore, go for walks, and lie by the pool, and even go to the casino at night. Even if she didn't gamble, it sounded like a scene worth observing, as high rollers from all over the world came to play.

She packed her bags that night, went for a last walk around the Place Vendôme, and left the hotel at eight o'clock the next morning, to catch her ten A.M. flight.

This time a white Rolls picked her up at the airport in Nice, which felt mildly embarrassing, but it seemed like fun in the spirit of the moment. Her room at the Hermitage looked out over the sparkling water of the Mediterranean. She noticed that there were huge yachts in the port, and promised herself she'd go for a walk there later to check it out.

She had lunch by the pool, then walked around Monte Carlo for a while. Every luxury shop in the world was represented there, and then she walked down to the port and stood admiring the many large boats moored in the harbor. There was a whole section of the largest yachts, with uniformed crews washing down the boats, or the owners and their friends on deck having an elegant late lunch. She was fascinated by it, then she saw the largest sailboat among them. A sleek beauty, with a flag she didn't recognize flying off the back of the boat. She was called *Lady Luck,* which made Maggie smile as she walked past her. The crew were diligently washing the boat, and the owner was nowhere in evidence. It looked like a wonderful life, sitting on the deck of those yachts. She walked back up the hill to the hotel after she left the port. It was a steep hill and a healthy walk.

She went swimming in the hotel pool late that afternoon, and took out her one slightly dressier dress to wear to the casino that night. They told her that it was usually pretty thinly populated until after midnight, and lively after that. So she ate dinner late at her hotel, and at twelve-thirty, she walked the short distance to the casino. As the concierge had told her, there were lots of people getting out of chauffeur-driven Rolls-Royces, tourists in evening clothes. She heard Russian, Arabic, Chinese, English, and French all around her, as well as a little German and some Italian. It looked like a tiny city mostly for the rich, and since it was a tax haven where residents didn't pay taxes, it was a magnet for people with a great deal of money. She saw several Ferraris pull up too, and beautiful women in evening gowns getting out. When she walked into the casino, she saw that most of the tables were full. It looked like a busy night, it was Saturday, and everyone was out.

She stopped at the roulette table for a while, which was fun but never seemed as exciting to her as blackjack or poker. She and Brad had gone to Las Vegas for some of his conventions. Neither of them were big gamblers, but it had been a lot of fun just playing the slot machines and watching the people intent at the blackjack tables.

Monte Carlo was infinitely more elegant and far more glamorous. The way people were dressed, who was there. Their whole demeanor, and the international mix among the crowd. She felt underdressed in her simple black dress, with her hair down. She noticed that all the women surrounding the tables and strolling through the casino were covered in expensive jewels. All she had was her gold wedding band and a small gold watch Brad had given her. She didn't feel as though she was competing with the women in the casino. They were all standing close to the men they had come with, who were gambling, and a few of the women were gambling too. Maggie felt like an invisible observer whom no one would notice, and was surprised to see several men staring at her. She was beautiful and didn't know it, and didn't really care. One of them invited her for a drink, and she politely declined. He had a heavy Spanish accent and was very handsome, but she was content to watch the gaming tables and didn't want to get tangled up with any man. She wasn't there for that. Just to have fun and see the life of the casino.

She noticed at one table they were playing blackjack with important-looking men in every seat. The stakes were high, and there was a huge amount of chips on the table. She wasn't sure how much it added up to, but she guessed at several hundred thousand euros, an almost equal amount of dollars. None of the players were speaking, the atmosphere was intense, and a few minutes after she began to watch, a youngish-looking man with silver-gray hair and a broad grin won. The croupier pushed an astounding amount of chips toward him, which he put in neat piles in front of him, and then started the betting again, as the men he had beaten groaned. He was handsome and looked much younger than the gray hair suggested. He appeared about Maggie's age, and had a youthful air. He looked vaguely familiar but she didn't know him. She heard him speak and he sounded American. He won the next hand too, much to everyone's dismay, but he lost a lot of money on the round after. It didn't seem to bother him, he remained good humored, and put a stack of chips in again. He looked up to where Maggie was standing and smiled at her. He had noticed her for a while and suddenly he called across to her with a look of surprise.

"Maggie Kelly? Is that you?" She was startled to hear her maiden name and nodded as he laughed. Suddenly she realized who it was, as her eyes grew wide in disbelief. It was Paul Gilmore, her high school love who had gone off to race motorcycles and later cars. She hadn't seen him in thirty years, he had disappeared into the mists of another life. She remembered how dangerous and wild her mother had thought him, and her dire predictions about him, and now here he was, winning and losing a fortune at the high-stakes table in Monte Carlo. She remembered how poor he was when they were in school and the shabby cottage he lived in with his mother. It was obvious he had done well. She remembered his saying he would be rich one day, and apparently he was. She vaguely recalled hearing that he was a famous Formula One driver, but his life was light-years from hers by then, and she was happily married to Brad. He wasn't interested in car races and Paul Gilmore was off her radar, and now suddenly he was smiling at her as though he had never left.

He had the aura of a rich man, and had the same dazzling smile as when he flew past her on his skateboard at seventeen. He beckoned to her as he picked up a hand, and she made her way quietly around the table to stand behind him. Then the chair next to him became vacant, and he whispered to her to sit next to him and bring him luck. His eyes were full of mischief and he almost looked the same, except for the gray hair.

"You've been doing fine without me," she whispered as she sat down, and made no comments as they played. Paul lost again, but not as much, and again didn't seem bothered by it. He filled his pockets with the vast amount of chips he had left, and stood up to cash them in.

"Bonsoir, Monsieur Gilmore," the croupier said. Paul left the table and Maggie followed him. He stopped immediately and gave her an enormous hug. She remembered easily how close they had been and how much she loved him.

"What are you doing here?" he asked her.

"I'm on vacation," she said, slightly embarrassed. It was too much to explain, without sounding pathetic.

"Are you alone?"

She nodded, suddenly feeling seventeen again. She had turned eighteen while they were dating. He was slightly older than she was, forty-nine now, and she was forty-eight. He still had a handsome boyish face, and the silver hair made him look sophisticated, but it was still Paul, no matter how far life had taken him from their humble beginnings. No one would have guessed it to look at him now. He had the appearance of a man of substance, accustomed to the fast life. "Come and have a drink with me," he said, visibly happy to see her. He cashed in his chips and put the money in his pocket, then led her to the bar. He couldn't take his eyes off her, as though she were some kind of mirage.

"You haven't changed a bit," he said, still beaming at her, and she laughed.

"You must be blind. I wish that were true."

"How long has it been?"

"Thirty years."

"We have a lot of catching up to do." He ordered champagne for both of them. "What are you doing here? Do you live in Europe?" he asked. She laughed at the thought and suddenly wished she did. He seemed so worldly and sophisticated, she felt like a hick next to him.

"No. I live in Lake Forest, Illinois. I'm just here on vacation." She tried to make it sound ordinary, although it wasn't for her, and she was acutely aware of how plain her dress was, and how simple she looked compared to the other women in the casino. When they had known each other, he had lived in that awful cottage, dirt poor, racing motorcycles, and she had had a stable home with Harry and her mother, who hadn't approved of him. He appeared to have done well in thirty years. Everyone in the casino seemed to know him and smiled when they saw him.

"Why are you here alone? You're married?" She was wearing her wedding ring. He knew nothing of her life since he'd last seen her. He had never gone home again, except for two days when his mother died, not long after he won his first big race. He had lost touch with everyone from his past.

She shook her head with a serious expression when he asked if she was married. "No, I'm not," she said simply.

He pointed to the ring with a quizzical expression. "Divorced? Bad guy? I remember how much your mother hated me."

Maggie grinned at the memory. "She thought you were wild and dangerous, and said you would break my heart." But he hadn't, they had parted on good terms when he left right after they graduated. She went to college, and he went to Southern California and Mexico to race. "No, I'm not divorced, and he was a great guy. We loved each other and we have a son. We were in a plane crash last December, and he died."

"Oh God. I'm sorry, Maggie. Was he flying his own plane? I fly too. That hits close to home." She smiled at the question, his life was obviously a lot more extravagant than theirs, and worlds apart.

"No, it was a commercial flight, from Chicago to New York. We wound up in the Hudson River in a snowstorm. Forty-nine people died and he was one of them."

"What rotten luck." He looked sympathetic and sad for her. She was still beautiful and too young to be a widow.

She nodded, there wasn't much more to add, except that it had nearly killed her and this was the first trip she'd ever taken alone, which she didn't want to say.

"What about you? Married? Kids?" she asked him.

"Twice and none," he answered with a grin. "I've been divorced twice, no kids. My exes tell me that my lifestyle is not compatible with marriage. Formula One racing, I climbed Everest ten years ago, helicopter skiing. I still like the scary challenges, women don't. Not in a husband anyway. And it never seemed right to me to have kids, given the things I like to do, so I never did. It wouldn't be fair to them."

"So you haven't changed." She smiled. He still liked all the high-risk, dangerous activities, her mother had been right. But she admired him for being responsible and not adding children to the mix. And his wives had bailed. "Where do you live?"

"All over the place. Paris, London, I have an apartment there. In Paris, I have a permanent suite at the Ritz. I have an apartment here too," he said.

"I just stayed at the Ritz," Maggie said.

"I spend time in Switzerland too. New York occasionally. My

work goes with me, so I can live pretty much anywhere." He seemed totally at ease and comfortable in his own skin. And he looked delighted to see her again. "How old is your son?" He wanted to know everything about her.

"He just started college in September, at Boston University." He understood better now. She was trying to find her way, and totally alone. Her husband had died, her son was gone. He felt a pang of deep sorrow for her, but she was brave and honest as she gazed at him. She always had been, and she looked no different to him now. "This is my first trip alone, and first trip to Europe," she confessed.

"What did your husband do?" He wondered what kind of man she'd married.

"He owned a family accounting firm."

"Do you work too?" He could just imagine it, they had had a wholesome, clean-cut, simple suburban life, and the bottom had dropped out of her world when her husband died.

"I worked for my husband's father before we got married, and I haven't worked full-time since our son was born. I'm trying to figure all that out now, about what to do next." She didn't look depressed about it. She looked like a newborn in some ways, trying to learn everything at once. It was sweet and it touched him. She seemed very pure and unspoiled, unlike the women he knew and was used to now. He admired her all the more for coming to Europe alone, which must have been daunting for her. She didn't seem like she was looking for a husband, in her austere, plain black dress. Its simplicity somehow highlighted her beauty. There was nothing to distract from her perfect figure, and flawlessly lovely face. He thought she was a hundred times more striking than all the painted dollies in the room, half of whom were expensive hookers, which he knew Maggie didn't realize, though he did. He was used to seeing them and could spot them with ease.

"I have a boat here. Would you like to come sailing with me tomorrow?" he asked her simply, and she nodded.

"I'd love it." He had been her high school sweetheart, and it was fun seeing him again. "I heard that you were a famous Formula One racer, but somehow I don't think I really connected the dots. I was living our quiet life in Lake Forest and that seemed very unreal." She understood it better now, seeing him in this setting and how people reacted to him. He was a very big deal. "Do you still race?"

"I do. Just not as often. I do the big races for my sponsors. And in case you're wondering if I'm an arms dealer, or a drug dealer, I'm not. I did well with racing and other dangerous pursuits, and invested intelligently. The more dangerous the sport, the higher the pay. And it does pay off very nicely. Most of the time, I follow my investments now. I have a contract to race when I want to. I pick and choose the races around the world. I don't have a home life anymore, but no one is complaining about the risks I take either. It's a trade-off. Freedom is addictive after a while, just like danger is. I'm hooked on the adrenaline rush." He said it with the same mischief in his eyes that she remembered from thirty years before. And he was honest about himself. He had been as a boy too. He'd never lied to her, and was clear about his priorities, even then.

"You always were hooked on that," she reminded him. "That was what my mother objected to, since my father was a fly junkie and it killed him."

"What happened to your brother?" he asked her. "He was such a cute kid. And a pain in the ass occasionally."

"He was. He died in Iraq, at twenty-three. He was a Navy pilot. It killed my mother. It took a while, but she never recovered. I married Brad right after that. I know being married to an accountant doesn't sound glamorous, but he was such a good man, and I wanted a safe life. I knew I'd have it with him. We were happy. And the irony is that he never took a single risk. We went to New York for a two-day trip, to an accounting convention, and the plane crashed. So I guess you never know how it's going to turn out, even if you're with the safest guy on the planet." And some men, like Paul, got away with taking all the risks. So far anyway.

"That's not fair." He was surprised she was still standing after losing her father, her brother, and now her husband, but Maggie had always been like that. Brave and determined. He knew she'd be okay now, but it must have hurt like hell.

He walked her back to her hotel then, and told her he'd pick her up at ten the next morning to go sailing. She smiled when she looked up at him and thanked him. She was thinking of him at eighteen, and what a sweet kid he was. How he had befriended her when no one else did. "That'll be fun." It was so odd to have run into him here and she was happy she had.

"And no scary stuff, I promise. Just a nice, tame day sail." He had never tried to frighten her, he saved all the high risks for himself.

"I'm looking forward to it." She went to her room thinking about him. Once she talked to him, he didn't seem to have changed much, no matter how sophisticated he looked. He was still so appealing and so profoundly nice, but her mother had been right too. He liked everything dangerous, and had sacrificed two marriages to do it. Romantically, he was a good man to stay away from. But she had no intention of getting involved with him, and he probably wouldn't want to either. They were just old friends connecting for a minute. There was nothing dangerous about that. It was just a funny quirk of fate that they'd run into each other. An odd coincidence, with no risk involved. He was just a reminder of a sweet memory from the past.

Chapter 6

Paul picked her up the next morning in a pale blue vintage Lamborghini that was almost a work of art. He drove her down to the port at full speed, chatting with her, and stopped next to an enormous sailboat. Suddenly, she realized that it was the one she had admired the day before. The *Lady Luck* was Paul's boat.

"I saw this boat yesterday." Maggie grinned at him in surprise. "She's beautiful."

"I love her," he admitted. "I've had a few boats, but I only love this one. She was built in Italy. I keep her here. She's registered in the Cayman Islands for tax reasons, I like keeping her here. I spend as much time on her as I can. In some ways, she's home to me." He had apartments all over the place, but his boat was home. He had certainly grown up to be footloose and fancy-free, and lived extravagantly. It suited him. He didn't seem to be hurting, or grieving over his marriages. She wondered what kind of women he had married, probably flashy ones. They had both grown up so much in thirty years, and taken such diametrically different paths. But his seemed to be working well for him. Hers had too, until the crash. She was doing okay now. She was slowly getting back on her feet and trying to get used to being alone.

Their day of sailing on the *Lady Luck* was absolutely perfect. They motored out of the port, and when they were clear of it, the crew turned off the engine and sailed his spectacular boat, which glided peacefully through the water. He was an expert sailor, and took the wheel for a while. He had a crew of eighteen on board. They sailed fairly far off the coast, and then came back to eat lunch in a protected cove near Saint-Jean-Cap-Ferrat. As they sat in the outdoor dining area, waited on by two stewardesses, eating lunch prepared by a fabulous chef, he talked about his years of racing all over the world, climbing Everest, his thirst to conquer impossible odds, including his marriages. Her life had been peaceful and uncomplicated compared to his, and certainly not exciting. In many ways, Maggie found he hadn't really changed since their time together at seventeen and eighteen, despite the luxurious trappings. He was bigger and older and had more expensive toys, but the drive he'd had then was still the same, and she suspected probably always would be. And he was just as kind and gentle as he had been as a boy. She wondered if her father had been that way, endearing but thrill seeking. At nine, she couldn't have assessed it. She thought her father was a hero, but maybe he had been as driven to take risks as Paul was. She was grateful that she'd had the sense to marry Brad and have a quiet life for almost twenty years. Paul's unquenchable thirst for danger would have terrified her. But Paul was still alive, and Brad wasn't, so nothing was predictable, as Paul had pointed out. And oddly, she still felt the same attraction to Paul she had at seventeen, and she could feel that he was attracted to her too, but they had nowhere to go with it. They would be off to their own lives again in a few days, miles from each other, living different lives. It was obvious to her that he was thoroughly enjoying his life just the way it was. He seemed to have no regrets that he was divorced.

They were lavishly but discreetly waited on all day. The crew never intruded on them. There was a constant stream of food or drink if they wanted it. They swam off the boat after lunch, and laughed like old times, like two kids. She remembered what a good sense of humor he had, and how much fun he was to be with. She had forgotten that about him. He could make anything seem special, even when they were both poor, and teenagers.

"I was always impressed that you wouldn't sleep with me," he said after they swam, as they lay in the sun close together on sunbeds.

"I knew you were leaving, and I was afraid that if I got pregnant, I'd never see you again."

"That was smart of you. You were a woman of principle even then."

"Just not a risk-taker, like you." She laughed, and he grinned. When they got too hot in the sun, they went swimming again, and chased each other in the water like children. At sunset, they finally sailed back toward Monaco, and he looked at her seriously.

"What are you going to do now? Are you really going to get a job?"

"I have absolutely no idea," she said. "I don't know why anyone would hire me. I'm a great car pool driver, I make good pancakes and a decent meatloaf. Other than working in a diner, or driving an Uber, I'm not qualified for much of anything. I like to think I was a good wife, but who knows." Brad had been so easy to please. She wondered now if she had done enough for him. Maybe she should have done more.

"Did he leave you any money?" Paul asked her softly, worried about her. She nodded, but didn't say anything specific. "Do you *have* to get a job?"

"I can't sit on my ass for the rest of my life doing nothing. I'll drive myself crazy. I was thinking I might work in an art gallery or something." She still loved art in all its forms, although Brad had never been interested in it. He liked numbers.

"Why don't you come skiing with me this winter?" Paul suggested out of the blue.

"I haven't skied in years. I learned in college, but Brad didn't like it. He played golf with his clients, and baseball when he was a kid and football in high school."

"I go helicopter skiing in Canada every year. But I was thinking more like Courchevel, which is fancier and would be more fun for you. You could hit the bunny slopes, and I could ski the three valleys, which is fairly challenging. I don't have anyone to go with me. I'm between women at the moment," he said, looking boyish and mischievous, and honest with her. They were still friends, after thirty years apart.

"I'm not sure if that's a compliment or an insult," she said as she laughed at him, "to be invited as filler." They were still oddly comfortable with each other because they had been so close as kids. They still felt like teenagers when they were together. She had always been able to say anything to him and in a way, neither of them had changed. They were just older, and richer. His lifestyle was impressive, and his boat was fabulous, but he was still Paul, in spite of the luxuries that surrounded him, and she hadn't changed either. He wasn't a show-off in an obnoxious way. He just lived well. *Very* well.

"We could go skiing after Christmas," he persisted. "I assume you'll be with your son during the holidays."

"Yes, I will." She wouldn't give that up for anything. He was the main event for her, the only event now, and she wouldn't let anything interfere with that.

"You could bring him if you want."

She smiled at him.

"He has to go back to school then." She thought about it, and it might be fun to go skiing with Paul, as friends. Sooner or later, he'd be involved with another woman and she wouldn't have the chance. And she liked the idea of coming back to Europe. He would be fun to do things with. He always had fun.

"I'll be on the boat in the Caribbean during the holidays. I always send it over in the winter. It's great to have it there. And I have friends who show up. Would you meet me in Courchevel after the holidays, Maggie?" he asked her with the look of a cocker spaniel pleading for a treat, and she laughed at him.

"Maybe. You might meet the love of your life before that. If you do, my feelings won't be hurt if you cancel the invitation." She had no expectations, which made everything easier between them.

"I won't cancel it. And I met the love of my life thirty years ago," he said, suddenly serious. "I just didn't know it then. I was too young to recognize it until you were long gone, and I had no idea how to find you."

"What does that mean?" She was startled by what he said.

"Just because we didn't see each other doesn't mean I stopped thinking about you or loving you. I always have. Feelings like that don't just vanish into thin air."

"You could have found me if you wanted to. I didn't go far," she said. She couldn't imagine that he had loved her for thirty years.

"Would you have married me if I'd found you?" he asked her longingly. She looked at him squarely when she answered him.

"No. You were everything I was afraid of, and my mother warned me about. She was right. People who wantonly risk their lives the way you do, and are addicted to it, are dangerous for those who love them. I don't want to end up like my mother, dying young, with dementia, because the losses were too much for her."

"You're stronger than that," he said solemnly.

"I hope so. But I still wouldn't take the chance. It's too danger-ous. Brad never scared me or broke my heart. He died in the end, but he wasn't risking his neck or my heart when he did. You're dangerous, Paul. You always were, and now you have all the tools and skills to do it better. You're still racing, you go helicopter skiing. You probably still skydive and mountain climb and do all the other crazy things you did. You couldn't even afford it then, and managed it anyway. I can't do that to myself, or my son. He needs stability in his life, now more than ever." And so did she. She didn't want to give that up.

"He has you for that," Paul said thoughtfully.

"Yes, he does. And I'm not sure you'd be a good influence on him. He has some of that thirst for risk that my father had, and you do. I try to keep a lid on it, but I know it's there, just waiting to spring out." She looked concerned as she said it. She worried about Aden, a lot. She could sense her father's genes in him.

"I like him already," Paul teased her.

"If you ever invite him to do something dangerous with you, I'll kill you." She sounded like a lioness protecting her cub when she said it. He could see that she meant it, and he intended to respect it.

"If he has that in his DNA, you won't be able to stop him, though," he said wisely. She knew it too.

"I know that. I'm just hoping to slow it down a little. He plays ice hockey in college."

"People like us have nine lives," Paul said to her. "Like me. I'm still here." And Brad wasn't, but he didn't say it. He didn't have to.

"One day you use up those tickets. I don't want to be around for that." She was serious and he knew it.

"All right, if I promise not to jump off a mountain or kill myself on our ski trip, will you go with me?" He was determined to convince her, but she looked at him and shook her head. They had lost each other for thirty years and a day after he'd found her, he wanted her to go skiing with him. It seemed too soon to her, and he wanted to start where they'd left off, at eighteen.

"I might go skiing with you sometime, but if you don't behave, I'll leave."

"Behave in what sense?" he teased her. "Risk-wise or in other ways? You're all grown up now, Maggie Kelly."

"You missed the boat on that," she said gently. "I still feel married to my husband." He nodded. He could tell. She was still wearing her wedding band, which was a clear message. He planned to respect that too. He had never forced her hand before, and didn't intend to now. And despite growing up in poverty, he was a gentleman.

"Separate rooms," he promised her, and she believed him. He had always been nice about that when they were dating in high school too. He had never insisted, or tried to push her to do something she didn't want to do. "What are you doing for dinner tomorrow night?" he asked her, changing the subject.

"I'm flying to London tomorrow, for the last week of my trip." She smiled at him and he smiled back. They were good together, they always had been, even as kids. She considered him a friend now, not a romance, no matter how attractive he still was.

"I'm supposed to fly to London tomorrow too. I was going to delay it for you. Do you want to fly with me?" he asked, and she grinned.

"Sure. Are you flying the plane?"

"No, I have a pilot, two of them. You're safe. Will you have dinner with me in London tomorrow night then?" She hesitated and then nodded. The old attraction still wasn't dead. But she knew better now. She wasn't going to let him get under her skin, no matter how nice he was to her, or how much fun he was to be with. He was still the same Paul, addicted to risk. Maybe worse, since he had the means to indulge it in every way he wanted to, which made him even more dangerous now.

They pulled into port at eight o'clock that night, after a full day on the boat. It had been heavenly. He had a very pleasant life. He invited her to have dinner on the boat. They had a delicious meal, prepared by his excellent chef. A light pasta with pesto and fresh tomatoes, a salad, and lemon sorbet for dessert.

"What are you going to do in London?" he asked her. He liked talking to her, just like old times.

"All the tourist stuff." She smiled at him, unembarrassed. She wanted to see it all, just as she had in Rome and Paris. "I want to see the Victoria and Albert Museum, and the Tate, the Tower of London, the crown jewels, Westminster Abbey, the changing of the guard at Buckingham Palace. All the silly, corny stuff, like Madame Tussauds."

"I'd do it with you, but I have meetings all day. Where are you staying?"

"Claridge's. It's been a nice trip. I saw everything in Rome and Paris. A friend said I should go to Venice, but I'm saving it for next time."

"I hope that'll be soon."

"Do you ever come to the States?" she asked him.

"Not often. Only when I have business there," he said. "Would you come if I race in the States?" he asked, and she shook her head.

"I don't want to see you get killed."

"I won't. Nine lives, remember?" He said it like a true gambler. They always thought they would win, or they wouldn't take the risk.

"If that were true, my father and brother would still be alive," she said soberly. "I wish Brad had had just two lives."

"Fate plays a part in it too," he said gently. "I'm a good driver. I won't get killed."

"I hope not, for you."

"There's no one it will matter to, if I do. I've kept it that way, so I can do what I want."

"It would matter to me, now that we've found each other again. Even as a friend, I don't want to lose you."

"You won't," he said with certainty. He didn't want to lose her again.

They talked until ten o'clock, and then he drove her back to her hotel. On the way, he stopped at the casino and asked her if she wanted to go in. She looked shocked.

"Like this?" She was wearing white jeans and a white sweater and sneakers. "Will they let us in?"

"They'd let me in naked with a rose in my teeth. I spend a lot of time here," and a lot of money. He loved to play blackjack and it evened out for him. He won and he lost, in large amounts, as she had seen the night before.

She followed him into the casino, and much to her amazement, no one complained about the way they were dressed, although she knew there was a dress code. He took a seat at the blackjack table and pointed to the seat next to him. She slid onto it and watched him play. He appeared casual and relaxed, and bought a stack of expensive chips. He lost them quickly and then made a big win. He bet all of it, doubled it, and then lost it all, and stood up with a smile. He looked at Maggie. "The table's cold. Time to go home." She had a feeling that he had just lost and won thousands of dollars, and broke even in the end.

He walked her into her hotel. "I had a great day," he said happily.

"Me too," she said, smiling at him.

"I'll pick you up at eight tomorrow morning."

"Thanks for letting me hitch a ride," she said, and he left a minute later. It was nice being with him, and odd too. It was a flashback in time, with the benefit of everything she'd learned since. She wasn't sure how much Paul had learned. He was still risking everything, at the blackjack table, on the racetrack, and in life. She wasn't willing to do that. Her mother's words had stuck with her, no matter how appealing he was. But it would be fun seeing him in London. Now she had a friend to have dinner with.

She packed her bags, and got ready for the trip, and then lay in bed thinking about the day on Paul's boat. It had been fabulous. She wanted to call Helen, but didn't feel comfortable telling her, she might make too much of it. Aden didn't need to know either, that she had run into her first love. So for now Paul was her secret, just as he had been before, when her mother forbade her to go out with him, and she had anyway. She reminded herself as she fell asleep that men like him were a dangerous secret to have. Maybe even as friends. But she knew she was smart enough not to fall in love with him again. He was a wild one, just as her mother had said. But there was no reason why they couldn't be friends. And there was no one to stop them. They were grown-ups this time. Or at least Maggie was. Paul was never going to grow up, but he made her feel like a kid again. Seeing him was like a trip back in time to a very sweet place she had almost forgotten, and remembered now, like a warm summer breeze from the past.

Chapter 7

Paul picked Maggie up right on time the next morning. She had checked out by then, and her bags were waiting in the lobby when he arrived at eight A.M. and put her suitcases in the Lamborghini.

"I was worried you might have more luggage." He grinned at her and she laughed. The trunk was very small, and her suitcases just fit in it.

"I'm traveling light this trip. I didn't think I'd be doing anything fancy." She had decided to buy a dress in London for dinner with him that night. He had already seen the only proper dress she had. The rest was all jeans and slacks, sweaters, and a peacoat in case it got chilly. She hadn't planned to dress up.

Having seen the *Lady Luck,* Maggie was not surprised when she saw his plane, which was a sleek G5 jet, luxuriously appointed inside in beige cashmere and leather. It was supremely comfortable. This was not the way she had expected to travel, but it was undeniably pleasant.

"I feel very spoiled," she said, as a stewardess served them breakfast after takeoff.

"My tax shelters allow me to lead a good life. I have a complicated corporate setup. It's all legal, but it protects me from the IRS. And I discovered a long time ago that I like living well. I have no one to be responsible for, or to, so I can spend it however I want. The first thing I did when I made real money, in a killing I made in commodities," he said. He wasn't afraid of high-risk investments either, and they had done well for him. "The first thing I did was buy my mother a decent house, instead of that shit shack she lived in. My father never sent her a penny. She thought she had died and gone to heaven. She died a year later, but she spent her last year in a beautiful home. It was the least I could do for her." He had a huge heart, and was very generous, even when he had nothing. Maggie had forgotten that about him, but remembered it now. The story about his mother touched her, and confirmed her faith in him as a person.

They talked about other things for the rest of the flight. He was intelligent and well informed and good company. As soon as they landed, he started making calls. He didn't have time to talk to her on the way into the city. He dropped her off at her hotel with a wave, and she checked in and got a cozy, very English room with flowered chintz and an old-fashioned mirrored dressing table. She wanted to call Aden that afternoon. She hadn't spoken to him in a few days, and he hadn't called her either. She didn't want to hound him. She knew he was busy.

She took care of her shopping needs first. She went to Harrods and bought a chic black dress and a pair of high heels. Then she did a little shopping for Aden, so she'd have something to bring him from the trip. She bought him a navy blue cashmere sweater and a warm black scarf. She bought a red wool scarf for Helen too. It would be freezing in Lake Forest soon.

After Harrods, she went to the Tate Britain and spent several hours there. She had her driver take her past Buckingham Palace, and it gave her a thrill when she saw the royal standard flying, which meant that the queen was in residence.

She went to the Tower of London, and saw a fabulous exhibit of the Queen's jewels, and to Westminster after that. She was saving the Victoria and Albert Museum for the next day. And she had a proper English tea at her hotel when she got back. She called Aden and caught him between classes. She got Helen while she was on the way to pick up her youngest son at school.

Aden told her about ice hockey practice, and she asked about his classes. He seemed to like his professors, and he told her how much he liked Boston. There were so many colleges in the area that it was a city full of young people. He had met lots of students from other schools too. They didn't talk long, but he sounded good to her. She could always tell if he had a problem, but he didn't seem to at the moment. Helen asked her a million questions about Paris and Monte Carlo. She wanted to know everything. Maggie didn't want to tell her about Paul Gilmore and had promised herself not to. It would make it seem too important when it was just a chance meeting with an old friend. Helen would try to make more of it than it was.

"Why Monte Carlo?" Helen was surprised at that and had never been there on any of her trips.

"I saw a brochure for it at the Ritz, and it looked like fun. It was. I went to the casino, played the slot machines for ten minutes, and won a hundred euros."

"You went to the casino alone?" Helen was surprised, and then Maggie decided not to lie to her and make a clean breast of it. She had nothing to feel guilty about, but she felt awkward anyway.

"Actually, I ran into an old friend from high school I hadn't seen since we graduated."

"How fun. What's she like?"

"It's not a she, it's a he. He's just an old friend, but it was nice to see him." Maggie sounded casual about it.

"Bingo!" Helen said, sounding triumphant. "That's exactly how it works. Most people our age who remarry run into an old friend from college, or a high school sweetheart, and they reconnect. Usually online, like on Facebook. That's perfect." It was exactly the reaction Maggie had expected and wanted to avoid.

"I'm not looking for a husband, and I don't want to remarry," Maggie reminded her.

"What does he do?"

"He's a race car driver."

"That sounds glamorous."

"Until he gets killed," Maggie said and meant it. "He raced motorcycles when we were in high school. He upgraded after that. My mother warned me to stay away from him then, and she was right."

"Is he a nice guy?"

"Very, but it is what it is."

"Is he single?"

"Yes." This was precisely why Maggie hadn't wanted to tell her. She knew Helen would make too much of it and decide it was kismet or fate or something. Running into him in Monaco was just a coincidence, and she was telling herself that too. Once she went home, she would probably never hear from him again. She didn't think the ski trip he was offering was real either. It was still three months away, and something else would come up by then. Another girl or a business deal or a race or some death-defying challenge.

"Why don't you want to go out with him?" Helen sounded puzzled.

"Because my mother was right. Men who're in love with danger and high-risk pursuits are heartbreakers."

"Maybe he'd give it up for you. He can't drive race cars forever."

"Guys like him just find other ways to kill themselves. Believe me, I know the breed." But she had bought a dress to wear for dinner with him, and it was a sexy one, so she wasn't sure she trusted herself either. Men like Paul were so hard to resist. They were appealing in so many ways.

Helen said she couldn't wait for Maggie to come home and tell her all about the trip.

"I can't wait to see you too. I still have another week here. Actually, he brought me here. He let me hitch a ride with him."

"He *drove* you there?" Helen was impressed by that.

"No, he gave me a ride on his plane."

"He has a plane?" Helen was even more impressed.

"He has a lot of things. When I knew him he was dirt poor. He's done well in thirty years."

"It sounds like it. I think you need to reconsider."

"No, I don't. I'm not looking for a guy with money." She didn't need to. She had her own, but she didn't want to tell Helen that. She was still uncomfortable about it. "If I were interested, I'd want some simple, normal guy like Brad, but I'm not. I probably won't see this one again for another thirty years."

"You will if you want to. He sounds interesting."

"Why? Because he has a plane?" That annoyed Maggie. It sounded so greedy to her, and she hated women who hit on rich men for whatever they could get. She was in that situation now herself, as a potential target, but at least no one knew about the money. They had kept it confidential for exactly that reason.

"He's interesting because he's obviously been successful, and that's always attractive," Helen said matter-of-factly. "Clearly he's a smart guy."

"He acts just like he did when we were kids. It's kind of refreshing. We knew each other so well, we don't need to impress each other."

"Were you in love with him then?"

"Yes. Then. Not now." She hoped that would stay true. After this week they'd be thousands of miles apart anyway. He'd forget her. She was sure of it, and the ski trip he was pushing her about would probably never happen. She didn't want to make any commitment to him. She didn't want a man in her life. She was certain of it.

"Well, keep me posted. You've certainly had an exciting trip."

"I can see why you love Europe and want to spend a year living here," Maggie said wistfully.

"Jeff would never do it. He wants to stay in the States, doing the same things forever. I'll never get him out of here. Maybe you and I should go on a trip," Helen suggested, and it sounded like a good idea to Maggie.

"I'd love it, if you can get away." That was the problem. Her married friends never could. But the trip on her own had gone well and had proved to her that she could do it and even enjoy it. She wanted to go on another trip in the new year. Maybe with her son, if he was willing.

She showered and changed after that, and she was satisfied when she looked in the mirror. She had found a little evening purse too, and she put on the heels she had bought at Harrods.

She was ready when Paul arrived at the hotel. He called her room and she came downstairs to meet him. He took her to Harry's Bar, a club he belonged to, famous for its fine Italian cuisine. She loved the food and the jet-set atmosphere. All the men were extremely well dressed, in beautifully tailored suits, and the women were wearing designer cocktail dresses, many of them with a lot of glitter. It was a chic crowd, and Maggie hoped that the dress she'd bought was nice enough. Paul smiled when he saw her.

"I love the dress!" he complimented her. "Did you just buy it?"

She nodded.

"Today. Just for you," she added, and then was sorry she said it. She didn't want him to think she was interested or pursuing him. She wasn't, but he was so good-looking and the setting was so romantic that she found herself flirting with him, and he appeared to be thoroughly enjoying it.

He took her to Annabel's afterwards to go dancing, and by the end of the evening, it felt like a date to both of them. She was re-lieved when he told her with regret that he had a commitment the following night that he couldn't get out of, but he wanted to see her again the next day. She thought they both needed to cool off, but two days later, he looked like they had been apart for years when he saw her and said he had missed her. He took her to his apartment for a drink before taking her out to dinner. He had a fabulous penthouse apartment in Knightsbridge that was the ulti-mate bachelor pad, with every kind of comfort, a remarkable sound system, and some magnificent art. He collected Old Mas-ters. Maggie said she had never seen such a beautiful place, and she meant it.

"I don't spend much time here," he admitted, "but I enjoy it when I do."

He had three bedrooms in all, with beautiful furniture and art throughout the apartment. He said a decorator had helped him. In addition, he had a wood-paneled library, an enormous living room, a home office, a state-of-the-art kitchen, a dining room, and a small but perfect movie theater. Maggie loved the apartment. Everything he owned was elegant, luxurious, in great taste, and expensive. For an instant the memory of the dilapidated shack he had lived in crossed her mind. He had come a long, long way from there, but he was still simple and unpretentious. She admired him for it.

"Whatever happened to the cute boy on the skateboard?"

"I just bought a motorized one that goes thirty-five miles an hour," he said sheepishly.

"Let me guess," she said cynically, "you don't wear a helmet."

"How did you know?" He laughed guiltily.

"I know you. You think a helmet would spoil all the fun. It would lower the risk factor." She suddenly wished he wasn't so crazy, and such a danger to himself. It made him unsuitable for any role in her life, even friendship. She didn't need any more losses. One day Paul would miss the mark and lose the bet and something terrible would happen. It was inevitable. It made her sad thinking about it.

He took her home that night and asked her to lunch the next day, but she had a museum tour set up, so he said he'd rearrange his dinner plans. She had no idea what they were doing, seeing each other every day. She had three days left in London, and she was flying back to Chicago on Sunday.

She finally asked him about it the following night.

"I don't think it's smart for us to see each other every day. Do you?"

He looked disappointed.

"Am I boring you?" He seemed crushed, and she laughed at the question.

"No. I love seeing you. But then what? This is no more suitable for either of us than it was thirty years ago. You're every bit as exciting and fun to be with as you were then, but you said yourself the risk factor in your life makes you ineligible for a serious relationship. I don't want another heartbreak if something happens to you, and it will, sooner or later. So what are we doing? We're tempting fate here."

"Maybe it could be different this time."

"I married an accountant so I wouldn't have to deal with someone like you. I never forgot you either," she said honestly, "but we're not seventeen anymore. We know how the story ends. And I don't want to wind up like my mother. You're the role model for everything I was trying to avoid when I married Brad."

"You won't wind up like your mother. You couldn't. Let's just slow down a little, and take a breather. I have to go to Switzerland for meetings tomorrow. Have dinner with me when I get back on Saturday, before you leave. I don't want to lose you again, Maggie."

"I'm still mourning Brad. It hasn't even been a year yet. I don't want a relationship and I can't afford another risk-taker in my life." She had been saying it to him all week, but he didn't want to hear it. She was relieved that she was going home. She agreed to see him on Saturday for her last night, for old times' sake, but she promised herself that she wouldn't fall for him again. It was all smoke and mirrors with him, with a keg of dynamite under the mirror, concealed by the smoke. He would blow them sky high if she let him, and her heart and life with it.

She had a peaceful day without him on Friday, and felt back in control again when he picked her up on Saturday night in a silver Ferrari and drove her to a fashionable restaurant, where everyone knew him. She noticed that people recognized him wherever they went. And they were always happy to see him. He was such a nice guy.

"How was Switzerland?" she asked him, looking bright-eyed and cheerful. He was particularly handsome that night. She had worn her plain black dress in order not to entice him. She didn't want to mislead him. However much she had loved him at seventeen, she didn't want to love him at forty-eight. She was past being dazzled by someone who would be a colossal mistake. The boat, the plane, and his fabulous penthouse didn't change that. What she liked about him was who he was and always had been, not the trappings he had picked up along the way.

He told her he was going to Luxembourg the next day and had business there the following week.

"Maybe you are a drug dealer," she teased him. "You sure move around a lot."

"I have a lot of corporations. It's all legal, but it takes a lot of shuffling to avoid losing half of it to taxes." She wondered if he took risks on that front too, but was sure he had capable tax lawyers to keep him out of trouble. "I'm going to Hong Kong in two weeks. And after that, I have a race in Barcelona." She felt a little shiver run down her spine then, like a premonition. It was precisely why she didn't want to fall for him again.

She felt now as though he had been put on her path as a reminder of what she didn't want, and a challenge to make sure she could resist him. He looked sad as they finished the meal. She had loved seeing him, but he was far more dangerous now than he had been at eighteen, because he was even more appealing. The sophistication he had acquired in the last thirty years made him seem like a grown-up, but she knew he wasn't. He was still a wild kid, tempting fate and wanting to see how far he could push the limits.

He drove her back to Claridge's, and he looked at her as she was about to get out of the car.

"It's been wonderful seeing you," she said gently. "Take care of yourself. Don't do anything stupid."

"I won't," he promised her, which she knew meant nothing. He would do something stupid again and again until one day his luck ran out. It was part of his appeal, wanting to believe in the impossible with him. He leaned gently toward her, and kissed her. It brought back a flood of memories, as though it had last happened yesterday, like a perfume she had forgotten and suddenly remembered. She could recall perfectly how he tasted now, how he kissed her, and how badly she had wanted him, but still managed to resist him. She didn't want to stop kissing him, and they didn't until they needed to come up for air.

"I'm sorry," he said softly. "I didn't mean to do that."

"Yes, you did." She smiled at him, still out of breath. "You were never a liar before."

"Okay, so I meant to do it. I've been wanting to kiss you all week."

"Me too," she admitted. She had never lied to him either. "But we can't. It doesn't make sense anyway. Your life is here, all over Europe and Asia, and mine is in Lake Forest, a million miles from the life you lead."

"There's nothing there for you anymore," he reminded her, in a final attempt to hold on to her, although he knew he couldn't.

"Aden will come home for holidays," she said stubbornly.

"For a few years, until he gets a job somewhere else. Come back, Maggie. I need you. We still love each other." What they had was a powerful attraction, but she wasn't convinced it was love.

"There's no room in your life for someone like me," she said, "and you know it too. You want me to give you stability, so you can turn my life upside down. That's not fair." He didn't answer her then, he just kissed her again, and she could feel all her resistance evaporate. She knew that if she didn't get out of his car, she would wind up in bed with him before the night was over and she'd regret it later. She kissed him one last time, and then without saying a word, she opened the door and got out, and he didn't stop her. They had entered a time warp for a week, in Monte Carlo and London, but now she had to let go and return to her real life, alone. She waved to him and disappeared into the hotel without looking back. He wanted to rush in after her, but he didn't. He knew that now, if he truly loved her, he had to let her go. And she knew it too. He drove away, blinded by tears. It was the hardest thing he'd ever done. He knew for certain this time that there would never be anyone like her in his life again.

Chapter 8

Traveling west in daylight hours, Maggie was awake for most of the flight from London to Chicago. She ate lunch, watched a movie, and closed her eyes for a while, but she kept thinking of Paul no matter how hard she tried not to. He was like background music in her head. She remembered each time she had seen him in Monte Carlo, the time they'd spent on the boat, and every moment they'd spent together in London. The vacation in San Francisco, Rome, and Paris had been peaceful and productive. She'd discovered cities she had always wanted to see. It had freed her and made her feel strong and independent. She had found her own footing again. It was the first thing she had done without Brad in almost twenty years, and she had proven to herself that she could. She had managed perfectly on her own, and even enjoyed it. It cleared her head and lifted her spirits.

But London and Monte Carlo were different, because she ran

into Paul. It had seemed fun and exciting at first to see him after so long, and revive cherished memories of her past, before Brad was even part of her life. It was like revisiting her youth, and she could no longer tell if what she felt for him was the echo of a distant time rekindled, or if it was what she felt for him now. The memories and the present reality were hard to discern and untangle. Every time she looked at him she saw the boy she had loved at eighteen. He hardly seemed any different now, other than the extravagant trappings that surrounded him, which meant nothing to her. She cared about Paul, both the boy and the man.

There was no option to go back to Brad now. She loved all of him without reserve, and could hold him close in her heart and mind, but she could never touch him again. Being with Paul was an alluring possibility, a choice she could make if she wished to, and a road she knew would be fraught with danger at every turn. Her mind shrieked *Run!* while her heart longed for his return. The last days of the trip when she was with him were a double-edged sword. The thought of it sliced through her again and again on the flight home.

She had been gone for four weeks in all, and was returning three weeks before Thanksgiving. She couldn't wait for Aden to come home. She needed to see him. He was the present and the future, where her responsibilities lay, and her strongest link to Brad. She wanted to hang on to the present, and all that was real in her life to keep the past at bay. She'd started having nightmares again in

London, which she hadn't had on the earlier part of the trip. She thought it was guilt tormenting her again, this time for being attracted to another man. She had mixed feelings about that too. She didn't want to be with anyone after Brad, out of loyalty to him. And even if she would feel different one day, it was still too soon. The first anniversary of his death was looming in six weeks, which she thought might be causing the nightmares too.

In fact, the decision about Paul had been made thirty years before, and she knew she had made the right one. With the life choices he had made, Paul hadn't changed. If anything, he was more addicted to risk than before.

She hoped that Paul wouldn't call her or try to get in touch with her in some other way. She was shocked by how easily she had melted into his arms and wanted to be there. It took all her resolve not to send him a message before she left. He hadn't called her that morning before her flight either. She was ready to put him back into ancient history, but each time she did, he popped into her mind again, like a jack-in-the-box she couldn't close. He refused to disappear from her thoughts, and she could still feel his lips on hers.

She was exhausted when she got off the plane, claimed her bags, and went through customs in Chicago. She'd booked a car to take her home. She was shocked by how cold it was. Winter had already begun to creep in, which suited her mood as she rode home to her empty house. But this was her turf now, not Paul's. She had given him all her contact information in Monaco, and hoped now that she wouldn't hear from him. She didn't want loneliness or grief, or the upcoming anniversary date, to color her decision or weaken her resolve not to see him again.

The house looked empty and bleak when she got there and let herself in. The woman who came to clean twice a week had left everything in order and put food in the refrigerator for her, but the house felt abandoned. You could tell that no one had been there. Aden's sports equipment wasn't lying in the front hall. There were no clothes scattered anywhere. Her mail was stacked neatly in the hall, but being there was like prying her heart open again, remembering that Brad was gone forever and Aden no longer lived there. It put her face-to-face in sharp relief with the reality that she was alone. Even Paul seemed like a dim memory when she walked in.

She dragged her suitcases upstairs to her bedroom and wandered around the house feeling lost. She texted Aden that she was safely home, but she didn't call anyone. She was no longer in a rush to see Helen. She would want to hear all about Paul, and Maggie didn't want to talk about him and stir the embers again. They needed to die now. She had been stunned by how easy it was to revive them, as though his memory had remained closer than she thought. Thirty years had vanished like mist as soon as she saw him.

She didn't bother to eat dinner, and it was a long sleepless night. She told herself it was jet lag, but she knew it was more than that. It was Paul, and her guilt about Brad had gotten stronger again the moment she walked through her front door, as though he were waiting there to reproach her. She still loved him, and knew she always would, but for a few days in London, Paul had filled her thoughts and her time, not her husband. She had finally fallen asleep when the sun came up. Helen called her three times after she got up, and she finally answered the last call. Maggie couldn't avoid her any longer. She had to say something.

"Are you okay? I've been calling you all day."

"I'm fine," she said, but she didn't sound it. "I was jet-lagged last night and couldn't sleep." The six-hour time difference with London was a plausible excuse, and Helen believed her.

"How does it feel to be home?" Helen sounded happy to hear her. She had missed her while she was gone.

"Strange. Hard. The house seems so empty without Aden." She hadn't really had time to realize to what degree. She had left so soon after he took off for Boston. It hadn't hit her yet, the way it did now.

"I was afraid of your walking into an empty house, although I could use a little of that here. You missed Halloween. We had kids in costumes in and out of here for days, Joey was in two parades at school, and wanted two different costumes," her youngest. Maggie missed those days and was happy she'd been in London. "So how's your old love? Do you think you'll hear from him again now that you're home?" She sounded hopeful, which set Maggie's nerves on edge immediately.

"I hope not. Sometimes the past is best left in the past. This is one of those times. Our lives are too different. And all the same things that would have made it wrong thirty years ago are still there and worse. I don't need to be widowed twice. Once is enough for me. A race car driver is not an option. I don't care how successful or famous he is."

"He managed to stay alive this long. He might make it to retirement in one piece," Helen said, sounding disappointed.

"He'll find something else dangerous to do if he ever does retire. He can't help himself. It's stronger than he is. It always will be. Skydiving, helicopter skiing, mountain climbing, the possibilities are endless and he loves them all. If anything, he's worse than he was as a kid. Maybe now he feels he has to prove something. He's one of the older drivers around now. And he has greater access to dangerous activities than he did when he was young and poor. He can do anything he wants now."

"It's such a shame. He sounds perfect," Helen said wistfully.

"Not for me. And apparently not for his ex-wives either. They both left him. One of them in less than a year." He had told her that in London. She was a model, eighteen years younger than he was. He said it had put him off younger women, but she wasn't sure she believed that either, if the temptation was strong enough. And Maggie had seen how women looked at him. He was a star everywhere he went. To his credit, she hadn't seen him look at any other women when he was with her. He hadn't been a cheater, even as a kid. And success hadn't gone to his head in that sense. But his career and love of danger weighed heavily enough on the wrong side of the scale.

"I'm sorry, Maggie," Helen said sincerely.

"I'm not. I averted disaster again this time."

"How did you leave it with him?" She was curious, and didn't want to let it go. He seemed like such an exciting option, and a way to fill Maggie's empty life now. She still had hard times ahead. And she was going to be so alone, with even Aden gone. In Helen's mind, a romance would have been a blessing. However loyal Maggie was to him, Brad wasn't coming back.

"We agreed on the last night that it was over." She didn't say "after we kissed for half an hour." Helen didn't need to know that. Maggie wanted to forget it herself. She had to, for her own peace of mind. "I think he was sad about it. He'll forget soon enough," she said, sounding hard for a minute. "Women must crawl all over him. People recognized him wherever we went. Guys think he's a hero. Women think he's hot. He's still good-looking."

"I looked him up on the internet. He *is* hot! He's great looking, and in the real world, he's still pretty young." At forty-nine, he was younger than Brad, and better looking, which wasn't what mattered to Maggie, any more than Paul's boat or his plane. They were just nice add-ons, but they weren't the main event for her. "I'm sorry I won't get to meet him. We could use a little window dressing around here." Her own husband was very good-looking, tall, athletic, with a great body. He kept in shape, worked out every day before work, and got up at four A.M. to do it. Helen worried about the women he met at work, who were twenty years younger than she was. She was two years younger than Maggie and the interns they hired at the agency were fresh out of college. Fortunately, most of them drove Jeff crazy. He said it was like hiring teenagers, and they weren't far from it. The agency had a game room for them now, and a candy bar, to keep them happy on their breaks. All the ad agencies and start-ups had them. Helen's boys loved going to visit him at the office so they could play. "Have you thought about what you're going to do now?" Helen changed the subject, but Maggie still didn't know. She had thought about all kinds of options, from volunteer work to going back to school for a master's in art, but nothing felt right so far.

"I thought about volunteering at the convalescent home here, but it sounds so depressing, talking to old people with dementia. It reminds me of my mother at the end. There has to be something more fun that I can do. Maybe something at the Museum of Contemporary Art. Even a class. There were so many great small art galleries in Paris. I thought about opening one here. But I'm not sure people buy art in Lake Forest. They go to the city for that, to give some weight to it." Helen didn't disagree with her.

"What about Brad's old firm?" Helen knew she had sold it.

"They don't need me. And I think it would remind me too much of Brad. Every time I've gone there, I expect him to walk out of his office, and say he was just kidding, and has been hiding for a year."

"I know. I felt that way about my sister. Every time I went home, I expected her to be there, for years."

"I've given myself till January to come up with an idea for work of some kind. It'll be here any minute, and I'm no closer to figuring it out than I was eleven months ago. It's hard to invent a career out of whole cloth. I didn't exactly have a booming career before I married Brad. I worked for him, as a receptionist at his accounting firm."

"You married the boss's son. As my mother-in-law says, it's nice work if you can find it." They both laughed and bantered back and forth for a while, and then Helen had to drop off a forgotten lunch at school for one of her boys. She seemed to be doing fine without her oldest son, since he was at Yale, but she still had the two younger ones at home, which helped. Maggie didn't have that consolation with an only child. And with a late baby, Helen wouldn't be facing an empty nest for another twelve years. Maggie envied her that. They agreed to have lunch the next day before they hung up, and Maggie was glad they'd talked. That way, she wouldn't have to rehash everything about Paul the next day.

It didn't help when three dozen red roses arrived from a local florist that afternoon. The card read "Thank you. I'm sorry. Love, Paul." They were beautiful but she was sorry he had sent them. It just prolonged things for another day, but it was thoughtful of him. She sent him a text to thank him, and was relieved when he didn't respond.

It took two weeks to stop thinking about him constantly, like giving up an addiction. The early days were the hardest. But by the time she'd been home for two weeks, Thanksgiving was only a week away, and she was busy getting ready for it, and Aden's return. It was going to be their first Thanksgiving without Brad. It would just be the two of them. She had taken out their Thanksgiving decorations, and she wanted to set a pretty table for them. She knew Aden wanted to see all his friends while he was home. The house would be bustling again, with kids arriving at all hours, Aden ordering pizzas for them, and all the boys watching football over the holiday weekend. Christmas was just around the corner, with Brad's anniversary date first, the anniversary of the crash. She hoped the media wouldn't hound her, looking for a follow-up to the story. There wasn't any at her end. She had read that some of the families hadn't settled with the airline, and were suing, and the airline was trying to keep it quiet.

She was finally feeling better by the time Aden got home. The nightmares had subsided again, and she'd only had one bad headache. The doctors had told her it would be that way, that the PTSD would flare up at times, particularly if something upset her, and then would calm down again. They had warned her that the flashbacks she had in her nightmares might continue for several years. But it was already significantly better after one. She was still aware of it at times, but not to the same degree, and she had stopped seeing the psychiatrist. There was nothing more she could do, and she thought Maggie had adjusted well. The trip to Europe was a good sign. And Maggie hadn't been back to see her since her return.

The house came to life instantly when Aden came home. His friends arrived within the hour he did. The kitchen was crammed full of young male bodies, voices calling to each other, laughter, doorbells ringing, you could hear them all over the house. Maggie loved it.

She was thrilled to see her son, and he was happy to be home, although he loved college and living in Boston.

The chaos only calmed down significantly on Thanksgiving Day, when his friends had to be at home with their families. But by nightfall they were back, louder than ever. It made Maggie smile listening to them. They all seemed to have grown up in the last three months.

The day after Thanksgiving, Aden was out with his friends all day. They were meeting up with some girls, dropping in at each other's houses, driving around to visit. Everything seemed lively, and Aden had brought home a mountain of laundry. She was even happy to do it. It made her feel useful.

On Friday night, a bunch of them piled into her basement playroom to watch a movie. They were still there, laughing and talking, when she went to bed. She liked it when Aden had friends over and she saw familiar faces from his school days.

She was surprised to see a lot of them back on Saturday morning, when she came out of the laundry room with an armload of clean clothes for him to take back to Boston. She noticed that they were watching a car race. It was in the heat of the race, and the commentator was excited. He was speaking over an announcer in another language, which sounded like Spanish. Instinctively, she stopped for a minute to watch it. Just as she did, she saw two cars crash into each other in a dramatic collision and then hit a third car. Within seconds, two of the cars burst into flames. As people screamed and others ran toward it, firemen leapt to the scene, and Aden and his friends were shouting and pointing at what was happening on the screen. It was a grisly scene as the drivers were pulled from the cars. One looked lifeless, and firefighters were fighting the flames as the crowd was roaring. Aden and his friends were agitated, and she hated watching but couldn't stop. One of the announcers said that a driver called Garcia-Marques appeared to be dead, another was carried away by paramedics, while the third one had escaped the blaze with parts of his driving suit on fire as he leapt from the car, and then had been surrounded by firemen and medical personnel putting the flames out. It was an impressive sight. Maggie was watching the screen as the boys stared in horror at what was happening and talked animatedly.

"Where is that?" she asked, setting the laundry down for a minute.

"Spain," one of the boys answered, still watching the TV, and then she heard his name, as the announcer explained that the man whose suit was in flames was the legendary Formula One driver Paul Gilmore. She felt frozen to the spot when she heard it, and her eyes were riveted to the screen with even greater interest. Paul was being led off the track, but still walking under his own steam and limping. He had taken his helmet off, his face was blackened. She knew that their driving suits were fire retardant, but the arms of his had caught fire anyway. The fire on him was out by then, and parts of his suit were charred. She sat down heavily in a chair as the boys continued to chatter, and the scene at the racetrack was utter chaos. One of the drivers had been officially declared dead by then, and the second one was said to be in critical condition from multiple injuries. Maggie's heart was racing.

"Gilmore is amazing," Aden commented to one of his friends. "He's the best driver I've ever seen, and I swear, he's walked away from some of the worst accidents in racing." Maggie had noted instantly his tone of admiration for Paul Gilmore. Most of the time she saw him watching hockey, football, or baseball. But he liked all sports to some degree. The other boys were talking about Paul then, and Maggie startled them when she spoke up.

"I went to high school with him. He's from around here, or he was then. I just ran into him in Europe. I hadn't seen him in thirty years." Aden looked stunned and impressed.

"You know him? You never told me that."

"I hadn't seen him since we graduated from high school. I was your age." She didn't say that he'd been her first love. It wasn't the sort of thing you'd tell a son, but more likely a daughter.

"Where did you see him in Europe?"

"I ran into him in Monte Carlo, and saw him again in London. He said something about a race in Barcelona."

"This is it," Aden said, his eyes bright from the excitement, and intrigued that she knew him and had seen him recently. "I'd love to meet him. Is he a cool guy?"

She smiled at the suggestion.

"By your standards, yes. He's as crazy as all those guys."

"He's the best driver ever. He wins almost every race. I've seen him cross the finish line with his car on fire. Nothing stops him."

"Yeah, I know that about him," she said, as she stood up to go upstairs with the laundry. She'd seen enough. Paul had survived another near-death experience. She'd seen it firsthand this time, and she hoped he was all right. The boys continued talking about him when she left them. After she put Aden's laundry on his bed, she went to the kitchen for a cup of coffee and found that her hands were shaking. She felt sorry for Paul. He had no one, no wife, no family. In his solitary life, who cared for him when he was injured or hurting? After the adrenaline rush, she suspected that he would be in pain from the accident. The announcer said they had taken him to a nearby hospital to check him, but he had made a miraculous escape. She wondered which life he'd used up this time. What number of his nine lives was he on?

She waited another hour, and then looked up the number he had given her on her phone. It was a British number, he had said it was the cell he used most often. She also had his email and a Swiss number for him. She called the cell, not sure if she would reach him, but at least she could leave him a message, that she had seen the accident on TV and hoped he was all right. She hadn't intended to call him again, but this was different, and she told herself that it wouldn't hurt anything to tell him that she felt bad for him.

It rang twice, and she was waiting for his voicemail when he picked up and answered in Spanish. He spoke it fluently from his motorcycle racing days in Mexico, which came in handy when he raced in Spain.

"Maggie?" He sounded stunned when he heard her voice.

"Yes. Are you okay? We were watching the race on TV. My son was with his friends. We saw it happen. Are you badly burned?"

"My hands are pretty toasted. The rest of me is okay. I broke six ribs, though. Occupational hazard." She was sure it wasn't the first time. "I have time off now anyway for the next few months, so they'll heal before I race again." He didn't sound worried about it, but she could tell he was in pain and having trouble talking. "I guess this doesn't help my case," he said, sounding glum.

"I'll give you a pass this time," she said gently. She felt sorry about the pain of breaking his ribs and having no one to take care of him. She didn't want to drive home the point on top of it. They both knew that his chosen career was dangerous, and he risked life and limb every time he went out there. "Are you going to be okay? Are they keeping you in the hospital?"

"They want to. I'm flying back to London in a few hours. I'll be fine. I'll take it easy for a few days."

"And then what?" She was concerned. He was real to her again since she had seen him recently. He wasn't just a memory or a dis-embodied voice from the past.

"I'm sending the *Lady Luck* down to Antigua. She's already on her way. I'll go down and spend some time on her when she gets there. They can take care of me. I can't move around much with six broken ribs." He sounded like he was having trouble breathing.

"I'm really sorry," she sympathized again, but at least he had somewhere to go to be nursed a little, and he could get there on his own plane.

"You're sweet to call. I thought I'd never hear from you again," he said sadly. He'd been elated to get her call.

"I wasn't going to," she admitted, "but I'm a sucker for guys with broken ribs and their clothes in flames."

He laughed and then cried out from the pain of it.

"Don't make me laugh." But she wasn't amused by what had happened. Watching the accident had been terrifying. Aden and his friends were used to seeing accidents like that during races they watched on TV, she wasn't, and the moment she heard that Paul was in it, she nearly fainted.

"Take care of yourself, Paul," she admonished him in a motherly tone.

"I will. You too." He remembered that she had a painful date coming up in a couple of weeks, and he knew that would be hard for her and her son.

"My son is vastly impressed that I know you, by the way. I told him I just ran into you in Monaco and London."

"Did you tell him that I'm the greatest guy you've ever known, other than his father, and that I've been in love with you for thirty years?"

"Actually, I left that part out. He doesn't need to know that."

"Let me know if you ever want to bring him to a race. I'll tell you if I'm going to do any in the States. You could bring him."

"I don't like the idea of his seeing people dying," which was what had happened in the race today. As usual, Paul had been the lucky one. The other two drivers weren't.

"That was really bad luck. I got off easily compared to the other guys."

"You're alive and survived another race. I'm grateful for that. I'll spare you my lecture. You know how I feel about it."

"What else would you have me do to make a living? Watercolors?"

"Maybe, if it kept you alive a few years longer. That seems worth it to me."

"I'd rather go up in flames than sit in a chair doing something boring for the rest of my life."

"I'm glad you didn't get your wish today."

"The only wish I have is to see you again, Maggie, and be with you. Do you want to come down to the boat? You could bring your son."

"We're going to be home for Christmas." It was going to be their second Christmas without Brad, and they knew it wouldn't be easy. Aden had promised to help her set up the outdoor lights the way Brad had always done, and to put up the Christmas tree with her.

"Let me know if you change your mind."

"I will. Thank you," she said politely, but she knew she wouldn't. Their traditions were more important than ever to them now. Paul didn't have any, since he had no family, so he didn't understand.

"Can I call you sometime?" he asked hesitantly.

"You don't need to," she said, which was her ultra-polite way of saying no. "I'll call to check on you if you like."

"Whenever you want. I won't bother you. Tell your son I say hello, if you tell him you called me." She doubted that she would. "And thanks for calling me, Maggie. It means a lot to me." She knew there was no one else to do it.

They hung up a minute later and she thought about him, and the crash she'd seen, all day. It was so exactly what she was afraid of. He had gotten lucky again. She was sure he must have had fifty lives, or a hundred. Nine seemed like far too few for the way he lived. He needed a thousand.

Chapter 9

Aden wasn't home from Boston yet on the anniversary of his father's death. It was the first one, and the day got Maggie in its grip and wouldn't let go from the moment she woke up in the morning. She had barely slept the night before, as images of the crash raced through her mind. She remembered what Brad had said to her when they were about to crash, and his face when she saw him drowning, too far away for them to get to him in time, as the currents had pulled him away from the life raft. She still didn't know how he had slipped out, but it didn't matter now. It had happened and they had to live with it.

She spoke to Aden twice that day, and he admitted that he wasn't doing well either. There was something so powerful and overwhelming about the actual date, as though the loss was different on that day than on others, which in fact it wasn't. But the date bound them to the anniversary of what had been the worst day of their lives, and it was all she could think of. There were no good memories attached to the day, unlike Brad's birthday. This was pure hell, remembering what had happened.

Phil Abrams sent her a card, and some of their friends had dropped off small bouquets of flowers. Paul sent her a text message telling her that he was thinking of her, but he didn't call. It was hard to guess the right thing to do in the circumstances, without intruding on something so personal. It troubled her that she had unwittingly opened the door to Paul again after his racing accident, and she didn't want to overdo it. He was being careful with her too.

A few days later, Aden came home from school for the holidays. He was staying just through Christmas, and then he was going skiing with friends in Vermont. One of his roommates had a family home there and had invited a mixed group to come skiing with them, and Aden was eager to go. Maggie had said he could, and didn't expect him to hang around with her all through the holidays, which would have been boring for him.

The first thing they did the day he got home was start setting up the outside lights to decorate the house, as Brad had done so expertly in the past. Maggie pulled out pictures of it, to copy exactly what he used to do. And they came fairly close. She stood on a ladder to help Aden as she had done with Brad. Aden tried to get on the roof, but it was too icy. They did a good job anyway. They even had a lit-up snowman in front of the house, and a Santa

Claus, which was their pièce de résistance. It was corny, but Maggie, Aden, and the neighborhood children loved it.

The next day they bought a tree and brought it home and decorated it with their favorite ornaments, including all the ones that Brad had liked. After the barren Christmas they'd had the year before, right after his death, this year was a vast improvement. She had bought Aden all the new ski equipment he wanted, and a racing helmet, which he flatly said he wouldn't wear.

"Good, then you can forget the trip to Vermont," she said with an iron look in her eye. "I'm not compromising on that. I know how you ski. I'm not having you get brain damage because you don't think it's cool to wear one. There are resorts in Europe where it's required, I've been told. People can die from not wearing helmets."

"They can die from slipping in the bathtub too," he pointed out angrily. "Do you want to forbid me to take a bath? Dad didn't wear a helmet when I skied with him."

"No, and he didn't ski like you. He was a very cautious skier, and hardly ever went, except to make you happy. He didn't go nuts like you when you hit the slopes." Aden had entered junior downhill ski races for a few years, and was an expert skier. He loved to ski as fast as he could. "It's up to you," she said adamantly. "No helmet, no Vermont. And don't lie to me and tell me you'll wear it, and then don't. I need to be able to trust you on this or you're not going."

He finally gave in the night before he was supposed to leave.

They'd had a lovely holiday other than that one argument. Even without Brad, their Christmas had been warm and cozy. Aden had gone skating several times with friends at a nearby pond where they skated every year when it froze over. He'd gone caroling, visited his old coach, Buck, and told him all about the hockey team at BU. He'd gone out twice with a girl he knew from high school who was in college in Boston too, and he had dated a few times there. And he had reveled in being at home in his room, in familiar surroundings with all his belongings. It felt good to be home, and Maggie had stocked up on all the foods he liked to eat. It had been a perfect Christmas vacation and he held his mother tight the morning he left to fly to Boston. He would drive up to Vermont with his friends the next day. He thanked her again, and hung out of the car and waved as he left, driven to the airport in Chicago by a friend's father. The roads were icy, and Maggie didn't like driving in those conditions, so Aden had hitched a ride with them. She stood in front of the house as long as she could see him, and then she went inside, grateful for the holiday with him, and sad to see him leave. He wasn't coming home again until spring break in March.

She'd had a text message from Paul on Christmas, wishing her a Merry Christmas and telling her that he was on the boat in Antigua, enjoying the comforts of the *Lady Luck,* and feeling better after the accident a month before. He said everything was healing well, and his ribs hardly hurt at all. He could even laugh now, which had been excruciating before.

She was putting some things away in Aden's room that night

when Paul called her and said he just wanted to check on how she was, since she had mentioned in her text response to his that Aden was going skiing. He had fully understood how much her son meant to her and how hard it was for her now that he was away.

It was nice hearing his voice. They had exchanged texts after his accident and on Christmas, but she hadn't heard his voice since she called him in Barcelona, after seeing him in flames on TV.

"What are you doing for New Year's?" he asked her, trying to sound casual, and she laughed.

"Going to bed with a good book. Brad and I never went out on New Year's. It's too scary on the roads that night. Are you still going skiing in Courchevel pretty soon?"

He laughed. "Not with six broken ribs. They're better, but not totally healed yet. I don't think I can ski for another month or two. I'm going to stay on the boat and relax. I don't have anything scheduled for the moment." And then he decided to leap in and see if his luck with her had improved. She sounded relaxed after the nice holiday with her son, and like she was in a good mood, now that Brad's anniversary date was behind her. He was hoping it might make a difference, but not sure it would. Maggie could be stubborn when she wanted to be. Once she had a point of view, or an opinion, she stuck to it, even at seventeen.

"What do you think about coming down to the boat for a few days, or a week or two, or as long as you like, just to relax and float around and get waited on?" He tried to make it sound as appealing and nonthreatening as he could. "Separate cabins of course. Just two old friends who enjoy each other's company. Besides, I'm not dangerous. I'm all taped up, and I can still barely move. You can push me overboard if I misbehave."

"I trust you," she said simply. He had never forced her before, and wouldn't now. She didn't trust herself quite as much, but she thought they understood each other. She didn't want a relationship with him, but they had a good time together, and they were both alone. She was well aware that it would be depressing now with Aden gone and the house empty. She had meant to sign up for some art history classes at the Museum of Contemporary Art, but hadn't done it yet. Floating around on the boat with him sounded immensely appealing, and she was feeling mellow about it. Being at home without Aden now was going to be hard.

"I'd invite you to bring Aden, but you said he's going skiing."

"Yeah, he left today. He'll be in Vermont till school starts in three weeks. Although if he knew you were inviting him, he'd probably ditch them and run. He's dying to meet you."

"I'd like to meet him too," Paul said, and had said it to her before. He knew how much Aden meant to her. He was her entire life now, and had been half of it before. "So what do you think?"

"Can I sleep on it?" She didn't want to do something impulsive and regret it later, and he had been careful to keep his distance and respect her boundaries since she'd seen him in London. She thought she could trust him on the boat, and it would be a lot nicer spending New Year's on a yacht in the Caribbean than in Lake Forest alone, shoveling out her driveway so she could go to the store.

She thought about it that night, and the offer was so tempting, it was hard to resist. Maybe they really could be friends. She hated to lose sight of him completely because she didn't want to date him. He seemed willing to accept the ground rules, and it was nice of him to offer. She called him the next morning and accepted, and he sounded delighted.

"How soon can you come?" he asked, sounding like a boy. "I can send the plane for you tonight, if you can come that soon."

"How about tomorrow? I've got some loose ends here."

"Perfect. Why don't you plan to be at O'Hare at ten? I can arrange a car for you if you want," he offered, and she smiled.

"I can manage that myself, but thank you. If I hang around you long enough, I'll become totally spoiled and helpless."

"I don't think there's any risk of that." He laughed. "You wouldn't let that happen."

"I'd try not to." She didn't want to depend on anyone. It was hard enough getting used to Brad being gone. She had promised herself that she wouldn't transfer that dependence to anyone else. She wanted to stand on her own two feet, and Paul respected her for it. She had always been a plucky girl, and had grown up to be a brave woman. She had proven it in the last year, since her husband's death.

She thought about his invitation again that night, questioning if she'd done the right thing, but she trusted him and they liked talking to each other. If it turned out to be a mistake, she'd come home. And Paul was seriously hampered now with six broken ribs. What harm could come of it? She sent both Helen and Aden a text, telling them that she was leaving for a few days, and they could reach her on her cell. They didn't need to know who she was with, or where, and she didn't tell them.

The plane was waiting for her at ten A.M. the next day at O'Hare as promised. She had already traveled on it from Nice to London, so, although she was grateful for the luxurious treat, she wasn't startled by it this time. The captain and both flight attendants, one male, one female, greeted her politely when she came on board.

They had long-range capabilities, so they flew directly to Antigua. The purser from the *Lady Luck* was waiting for her at the airport in Antigua with a van. They whisked her through customs, and she arrived on the boat shortly after, looking happy and relaxed in jeans and sneakers. The more she thought of it, the more she decided that this had been a great idea, and a generous invitation. Paul beamed when he saw her. He moved stiffly but came forward rapidly to hug her when he saw her arrive, and the deckhands took her bags to the spacious cabin Paul had chosen for her. He wanted it to be a perfect trip for her and it promised to be. They had no special plans, they were just going to float around the islands and go ashore when they wanted to. She'd brought a stack of books to read, since she hadn't decided yet how long to stay. She had no pressing reason to go back, other than the museum classes she wanted to take, but being on the boat was much more appealing than a dry museum class in Chicago.

The chef had prepared a plate of perfect tea sandwiches and iced tea for her as a snack. Being on the boat was luxurious and comfortable, and Paul loved being able to share it with her. It was the only gift he could think of to give her, to make her life more pleasant.

They sat talking until nearly dinnertime, and then went to their cabins to put on sweaters, since it got chilly at night. He observed no formalities there unless he had special guests, where it was required. With Maggie, he could relax, which he preferred.

They had a beautifully prepared dinner of delicate sole meunière and local seafood. They were at anchor off Antigua, which he liked better than being crowded in port with all the other boats, passersby, gawkers, and noise. Slightly off the coast, it was silent and peaceful. They sat for a long time after dinner talking some more, and then played liar's dice for half an hour before they went to bed in their separate cabins. He didn't make an issue of her sleeping in her own cabin, or try to seduce her. He just seemed happy to be with her, and didn't ask for more than that. As soon as she got to her bed that night, she was out cold, and slept until ten A.M. the next day.

When she came up on deck in the morning, Paul was reading the newspapers the crew had brought from shore for him, the sun was bright, and there was a gentle breeze so it wasn't too hot.

"My God, this is paradise," she said, smiling at him. "I don't know what I've ever done to deserve this, but thank you for having me."

He could see how grateful she was. And he was being careful not to romance her. He didn't want to scare her off. He was following her rules and respecting her boundaries.

They set sail a little while later, and sailed all day, before stopping near one of the small islands later that afternoon. They got off the boat and swam then, one of the tenders took them to the nearest beach, which was utterly deserted, with fine snow-white sand. Afterwards, they went back to the boat. Paul went to get a massage, and Maggie curled up with a book.

Each day seemed more relaxing than the previous one. They sailed around the local islands, anchored in port occasionally for a brief time to get supplies. And then they left the port and sailed again. The big sailboat handled smoothly and sometimes Maggie sat next to Paul at the wheel when he sailed it himself.

Their meals were exquisite and delicious. The crew were well trained and discreet, and Paul was wonderful company, and despite his broken ribs, he made her laugh with funny stories. He had become the perfect friend. She tried to make herself forget that she had ever been in love with him, and that they had kissed in London. She still felt the same attraction to him, but wouldn't allow herself to respond or act on it. She wanted to keep their relationship chaste, which seemed simpler to her. She did not want to be the girlfriend of a race car driver with all the terror that would entail, worrying about him before and during every race, and panicked that he'd get injured or worse. As friends, she told herself, she could maintain a safe distance, but almost imperceptibly, day by day, they got closer and more at ease with each other.

They had been in love as kids, and now they were totally comfortable companions as adults.

When Maggie texted Helen that she was going on a brief vacation after Christmas, Helen instantly had a suspicion that Maggie was with Paul. She didn't want to ask her and break the spell of whatever she was doing, or intrude. She waited to hear from her. And Aden was having too much fun with his friends to worry about where his mother was, or to ask. He knew how to reach her if he needed to. He thought maybe she had gone to a spa, which she had never done before, or that she was in New York.

On the day of New Year's Eve, they motored into port at Saint Barth's, spent a few hours there and then anchored just offshore, outside the port. Some of the biggest and most luxurious boats were there. They were mostly owned by Russians, who seemed to have cornered the market on huge boats. Even the *Lady Luck* seemed modest by comparison, although she could hold her own among the finest yachts, and she was very big for a sailboat.

"We'll be able to see the fireworks from here tonight," Paul told her.

She wore a simple white knit dress and silver sandals, and he wore white jeans and a navy blue blazer. She liked the fact that they were casual on his boat, and they were sailing just the two of them, without fanfare, formalities, or friends. She was completely relaxed with him, and he seemed equally so with her. Sometimes they sat and held hands as they watched the sun set, but she felt no pressure to do anything more with him. He had understood what she wanted and was willing to share with him. A deep loving friendship, enriched by their long history, but nothing more. It was the only way she could make her peace with his dangerous pursuits. She knew that if she slept with him, or became his woman, she would be crazed every time he raced, and terrified he'd die. This way it was his own affair. She would worry anyway, but she had no claim on him, and he had none on her. She thought it was the only way it might work.

At the end of the vacation, she would go home and pursue her own life and do as she wished. She didn't want him to die as a friend either, but there was no tempering what Paul did, or taming him. He was willing to live through broken ribs, or burns, or more severe injuries to do what he wanted, and she had to let him, and hope for the best for him. But she couldn't pin her future on him, or even count on his staying alive, given how he wanted to live.

Seeing him race in Barcelona had been frightening, especially when his car caught fire, and he emerged from the wreckage ablaze himself. She hadn't discussed it with him, and didn't intend to, but she knew he was still in pain from his injuries, although he was a good sport about them and never complained. He accepted them as part of his job, the way other people accepted late hours or demanding working conditions. He was willing to get injured and risk his life. In fact, he loved it. It was some sort of badge of courage he wore with pride. When she saw his body taped from shoulders to hips when they went swimming, she winced realizing the pain it must have caused him. And one hand was still bright pink from where he'd been burned. As a friend, she was trying to accept him as he was.

He was still hoping to ski in Courchevel next month and wanted her to go with him, but so far she hadn't changed her mind. She had two months to do whatever she wanted, before Aden came home for spring break in March. She still missed him terribly, but in exchange, she had enormous freedom. It would have been different if Brad was alive, she would have been with him. But now, Paul was helping her fill the time in the most agreeable and luxurious ways possible, more than she could ever have imagined. They were satisfying each other's needs for companionship, without altering each other's lives. It seemed ideal to her.

They drank champagne and ate caviar on New Year's Eve, and then lobster, and baked Alaska for dessert.

He smiled at Maggie as they finished dessert and he poured more champagne. "You know, I enjoy my life, but I never forget how poor I was. It keeps me humble. And if I ever lose it all, I'll make it again."

"By risking your life the way you have for all these years?" she said with a cynical look. "That's a high price to pay. You've earned all this with blood money. Your blood. Like in Barcelona. I hate to see you doing that." But she knew she couldn't stop him and didn't try. His dangerous pursuits were part of him. Although he didn't look it, he was still wild.

They sat in the comfortable chairs on deck and he put a blanket around her as they watched the fireworks. He glanced at his watch just before midnight. "It's almost here," he said with a smile, "a new year. I hope it's a good one for you, Maggie. I hope you get everything you want. You deserve it."

"You too." She smiled at him, and she wished him to stay alive for a long time, but didn't say it.

Two minutes later, on the stroke of midnight, with silvery fireworks exploding in showers of what looked like diamonds above them, he kissed her as he had in London, and this time she didn't stop him. It was too comfortable and too tender being with him to keep resisting their feelings for each other. And she didn't feel guilty about Brad now, which made a difference. She was here, in the moment, with Paul, and it felt right being together, however long it lasted, or didn't. They didn't want anything from each other, except to share this time. They weren't hurting anybody. And if the risks he took became too much for her, she knew she would leave him, and he knew it too. It was the unspoken agreement between them. She had made her peace with who he was, and thought she could live with it.

She kissed him then, and they stayed on deck for a long time, nestled under the blanket, until the fireworks stopped, and their kisses continued.

"Happy new year, Maggie," he whispered to her. "I love you."

"I love you too. Please try to stay alive for me this year. It's all I want from you," she whispered. And then she quietly followed him down to his cabin, where they celebrated a new year, and a new chapter of their lives together. For now, it felt like the right one.

Chapter 10

On New Year's Day, they sailed away from Saint Barth's, to stop at some of the other islands. She nestled next to Paul as they sat on one of the comfortable couches, and he pulled her a little closer to him. They both knew what had happened and what it meant. There was no one they needed to share it with.

"When am I going to meet Aden?" he asked, wanting to include him in their circle and not leave him out. "Why don't the two of you come on the boat in the South of France this summer?"

"He's planning to travel in Europe with friends in June."

"That's perfect. Come on the boat in July. Or you could come in June and Aden can join us in July." She liked the idea. She knew Aden would be ecstatic to meet Paul Gilmore, but she wasn't sure how he would react to her being involved with him romantically, and if he would view it as a betrayal of his father. She had to tell him about Paul first. "What about you?" Paul asked her. "How long can you stay now?"

"Since I haven't figured out a job for myself yet, I'm free until Aden comes home for spring break in March. What about you? Do you have to be somewhere?"

"In theory I'm still recuperating." He laughed. "The doctors in Spain told me to take it easy for four months. Not likely. I have meetings in London and Zurich at the end of the month, and a race in February. I have to be in shape by then. I'll start training in a few weeks," he said, looking relaxed. "Why don't you stay, if you want to, until the end of the month, and then come to London with me? You can stay as long as you want."

"When are you racing?" She wanted to leave before that. She didn't want to see it. And he knew better than to insist she be there. He knew how she felt about it.

"Mid-February in England, France in May, Italy in September. I have a race in China next year, and one in Australia."

"I think I'll miss those too." She smiled at him. Maybe not having to see him risk his life would work for them. Until the day that the worst happened. She still wasn't sure she would be able to endure it. But she was following him for now, with no long-term commitment. He understood the conditions and was willing to accept them to be with her.

"So you'll come to London with me after the boat?" She nodded. It was good enough for the time being. And Aden's spring break worked perfectly for Paul. He had some business trips planned then. He had given up the loan of the chalet in Courchevel. He wasn't up to that yet.

They had made their plans as far ahead as they needed to. She sighed that she hadn't brought city clothes with her for London at the end of January, and would have to go shopping again.

The next three weeks on the boat with him were like a honeymoon, and they both hated to leave when they met up with his plane in Antigua. They flew to London, and within hours he was tied up with conference calls and meetings with firms he invested in all over the world.

She bought just enough clothes to look respectable when she went out with him. They stayed home a lot, and he was doing deals in a dozen time zones, busy and awake at all hours.

They stayed at the Baur au Lac in Zurich when he had to go there, and she took long walks around the lake, and thought about the changes she'd made in her life in the past month, and even the past year since Brad died. Her horizons had broadened exponentially.

She called Helen when they got back to London, who said she'd been worried about her. Maggie had sent her regular texts, but they were somewhat cryptic.

"*Where* are you?"

"In London. I've been on Paul's boat since right after Christmas."

"Wow, how is that going?"

"Okay, so far. We're living day to day, which is the only way I can do this. I need to see what it feels like to live with a man who risks his life for a living. It probably won't last forever, but it works for now."

Helen admired her courage and willingness to check it out, given her history. But Maggie did love Paul. It made it worth trying to make it work, for both of them.

"When are you coming home?"

"In a few weeks. He has a race in February. I want to leave before that. And Aden has spring break in March, so I'll be home for a while. Maybe I'll come to see Paul again in April. And then Aden's school year ends in May. And he wants to stay home until he goes to Europe with friends in June."

"Complicated life. It sounds like a balancing act between Paul and Aden."

"It will be. And I don't know how Aden will feel about him. He may see it as a betrayal of Brad." She was prepared for the possibility and would face it when it happened. They talked for a few more minutes, and then hung up. Maggie promised to call her again soon. Helen missed her, but she was happy for her if Paul made her happy. Maggie still wasn't sure, but loved being with him every day. They understood each other, and he was a kind, loving man who knew her well.

As she spent more time with him, Maggie noticed that Paul didn't have many friends, if any. A few acquaintances on the London scene. All he had were people he did business with. The calls between Paul and his advisors developed a frantic quality in early

February. She didn't ask Paul why, and didn't want to be intrusive, but she noticed that he often looked stressed after the calls. There was a tension in him that he didn't always explain. He said nothing to her about his complex business dealings, and always told her everything was fine. He shielded her from anything stressful or unpleasant. She'd been through enough pain.

The race in the north of England was set for the twelfth of February, and she was planning to leave two days before that on a commercial flight to Chicago. The night before she was due to leave, Paul asked her to come with him, and be at the race.

"You know I don't want to do that," she said, frowning. He was crossing a line.

"I know. Just this once. You'll bring me luck. You don't have to do it again if you hate it." He didn't push her, but she could see that it meant a lot to him, so she agreed, and changed her flight to three days later.

She drove north with him two days before the race. She stayed in the background once they got there. He was busy checking out the car. He was as intense about his racing as he was about his business dealings all over the world. He did everything with passion, including loving her.

The day of the race, she woke with a feeling of terror. She hated being there, and was annoyed at herself for getting talked into it.

She stood grim-faced as the race began, her whole body tense until it ached. He had several near disasters on the track, scraped along a wall, tore off part of a fender, narrowly missed a collision twice. Yet in the end he won. But at what price glory? Maggie was drenched in sweat and shaking when he came to find her, beaming. He was filthy, and his broken ribs were still taped, but to him, every minute was worth it. It was what he lived for.

"It was great, wasn't it?" He smiled broadly at her and kissed her, but she didn't answer him at first.

"Great for you. Agony for me. You'll have to go to your races without me," she said, and he knew she meant it, so he didn't argue with her. He didn't want to upend the delicate balance they had established in the past two months, which seemed to be working.

"I understand," he said gently. They drove back to London, with his car on a truck, to be worked on at his warehouse close to London, where he kept all his race cars. They spent a quiet night together, without talking about the race after she congratulated him. They made love that night, as she clung to him desperately, and he felt guilty when she had nightmares all night, the worst he'd ever seen. She would fly to Chicago the next day. It was time to go back to her own life, check on her own investments, and get ready for Aden to come home in three weeks. She needed to be on her own turf, sleep in her own bed, and be away from Paul for a while. Everything about him was intense. She kissed him when she left and was happy to go home to her simple life in Lake Forest, and be by herself.

She could hardly wait to see Aden. When he came home, it felt like Christmas all over again. He knew that some of his friends would be there, and others wouldn't. He saw as many friends as were there, and had a couple of quiet dinners with his mother.

The second night he ate at home, she told him about Paul, and braced herself for his reaction.

"Paul *Gilmore*? The race car driver? Are you serious? That's sick, Mom!" She thought he meant it literally and her face went pale, only to discover from his comments a minute later that "sick" was the new jargon for "cool in the extreme." For a few minutes, he had panicked her. Then they both got serious. "Are you in love with him?" It was a reasonable question, and she wasn't sure what to answer.

"I was very much in love with him as a teenager, when I was seventeen. I loved him like a kid then. And I love him differently now. I like being with him, we understand each other and know each other well, even though there was a thirty-year gap before I saw him again last September in Monte Carlo. I loved the life I had with your father. I don't like the life of being with a man who needs to risk his life every day in order to feel alive and justify his existence, and who thinks that's fun."

"That's how he makes his living, Mom. He's a legend. He's one of the most important drivers who ever lived. He's broken nearly every record." Aden was vastly impressed by him, and wanted a hero in his life, which worried Maggie too.

"That's hard on the people who love them. That's why he isn't married and doesn't have kids. Racing is more important to him. I wouldn't want to live that way forever, but it works for now. He's a very kind, generous man, and I think you'll like him. I like him too. I even love him, though differently from your father. I loved the sense of safety and security your dad gave me. That's important to me. So where this is going? I don't know yet. Maybe nowhere." She was trying to be as honest as she could with him, although he was young to understand it.

"Are you having fun with him?"

"I am," she said, and smiled.

"Then why don't you just enjoy it and see what happens? Why do girls have to get so serious all the time?" She laughed. He sounded like a man.

"Are you having problems with that?" She was curious about his love life. He didn't tell her as much now that he was in Boston.

"I don't know. I've been seeing this girl, and she always wants to know where it's going. I don't know where it's going. I don't want to worry about that now. I just want to have fun with her. She acts like she wants to get married. I'm too young for that."

"Yes, you are. And I'm not interested in getting married either. I just wanted you to know that we're dating."

"Can I tell people?" he asked, smiling widely. He had had none of the bad reactions she had feared. He was being very mature about it, maybe because of who Paul was.

"Yes, you can. It's not a secret."

"Wait till I tell the guys you're dating Paul Gilmore." They both laughed at that. Paul was a star in Aden's world.

"He invited us both on his boat in the South of France in July. It's a beautiful sailboat."

"I'm coming!" Aden said immediately. Problem solved. She had heard horror stories of children his age and older objecting vehemently to their mothers dating at all, but Aden had no problem with it. And the fact that she was dating a legendary race car driver was even better. There was a bit of stardust in Aden's eyes. She just didn't want Aden emulating Paul and wanting to race one day. She had already said that to Paul many times. She didn't want him glamorizing it to Aden, or doing anything dangerous with him. She had a feeling that Aden would find his way to his own dangerous pursuits soon enough. He had the DNA for it on her side. She was enormously relieved by his sensible reaction to her news, and he didn't seem at all surprised that she was dating. It had been over a year since his father died.

She called Paul and told him about it late that night, when Aden was out. It was late enough to be morning in London.

"I thought he'd be okay with it, or at least I hoped so. But you can never tell with kids," he conceded.

"I think he's hungry for male company, or male guidance. His father has been gone for fifteen months now. He hangs around a lot with his friends' fathers, and he was very close to the coach last year in high school."

"I'd like to spend time with him when I'm around," Paul said softly. "We'll have fun together on the boat in July," he promised her, and she was touched. She noticed that he sounded tired, and he had been stressed lately. He never discussed his business problems with her. She knew he had corporate entities in several countries and they seemed very complex. Her own financial setup was much simpler and her investments had done well in the past year.

She had gathered that Paul liked the high stakes in his financial affairs too. His theory was that you only made the big money with big risks, but you lost big too. It was the exact opposite of how she invested her money. She wanted to hang on to as much of it as she could, and have it grow if possible, for Aden to have in later years. Paul invested as he lived, on the razor's edge, with his money, with his life, with his career. Danger was always the principal ingredient, and she didn't want him sharing that with her son. She knew where it could lead.

Aden went back to Boston after spring break. He would be home in two months for the summer. His first year at BU had gone well. His grades were reasonable, though not extraordinary, but he had been through a lot of difficult changes in the past year. And he had enjoyed playing on the junior hockey team. He was looking forward to discovering Europe with his friends in June. And now he would be joining her and Paul on the boat at the beginning of July. It was going to be a sharp contrast to his travels by train with a backpack around Europe. He and his friends were planning to visit Spain, France, Italy, Scotland, and England. Paul was talking about going to Corsica and Sardinia with the boat. There was so much she wanted to share with Aden now. He had grown wings of his own in the past year, and she wanted to spend time with him while she still could, before he flew too far in his own skies and no longer wanted to be with her. She knew that time was coming, and was already near.

She hadn't spread her own wings and found an avenue to pursue career-wise yet. She still wanted to, but dividing herself between Paul's world and her own, she wasn't in either place long enough to get a job. She was afraid to start her own business, and she was in Europe so much with him, she couldn't offer any employer enough time to be useful to them. But the time she spent with Paul was important to her too. The idea of working for or owning an art gallery appealed to her, but she wasn't around anywhere long enough to run it.

She said something about it to Helen, who suggested she sell art on the internet, and Maggie liked the idea. She wanted to explore it further, maybe over the summer. She could have a gallery online. It might be the perfect solution for her. She wanted to have her own activity. She didn't want to be a hanger-on in Paul's life with nothing to do. She wanted to be her own person, with her own interests and pursuits.

She tried to talk to Paul about it after Aden went back to school, but he seemed distracted and short with her every time they spoke. She thought he might have a big deal of some kind cooking. Whenever she called him lately he was on a conference call, or told her he'd call her back, and then didn't for hours, or not at all. Until then, he had been far more attentive. She was thinking of meeting him in London in April, before Aden came home for the summer in May. She wanted to visit Paul at the right time for both of them, and not just land on him, but he didn't have time to talk to her when she called him about dates. She hadn't spoken to him in two days, which was unusual. She wondered if he was traveling to one of the other cities where he had either corporations or investments.

She was mildly annoyed by his two-day silence when Helen called her with a strange tone in her voice.

"Have you seen *The New York Times* today?" Helen asked her.

"No. Why? I usually only read it on Sundays. The rest of the time I just read bits and pieces online."

"It's on the front page. About Paul." She sounded somber. "'The famous Formula One driver, international investor, and bon vivant, Paul Gilmore, is under investigation for tax evasion, fraudulent activities, and the use of illegal offshore corporations, involving many millions of dollars.' And it says that his apartment in London has been seized by the British tax authorities who are investigating him too. His accounts in both countries have been frozen pending further investigation. The ownership of his yacht and his corporate jet are in question, and they may be seized as well." Helen sounded shocked.

"Oh my God." Maggie hung up seconds later and read the article herself online. She had no idea what had happened. He hadn't said anything to her. As soon as she finished reading the *Times* article, she called him, but all she got was his voicemail. She realized that he couldn't be at the London apartment if the government had seized it. The question now was where was he and what had he done, and whether or not she even knew him. Her heart pounded as she called him a second time, and got voicemail again. Three hours later, after trying to reach him everywhere, she still hadn't found him. Paul seemed to have vanished into thin air.

Chapter 11

Twenty-four hours after the call from Helen, Maggie still hadn't heard from Paul, or been able to reach him. She hadn't spoken to him in three days. Aden had seen the article by then too, and called his mother immediately.

"What's going on, Mom? Is all that stuff true? Do you think he'll go to jail?" Aden hadn't met Paul yet, but he idolized him and hated the idea that he might be a crook. So did Maggie. She was worried about it too.

"I don't know," she said. "All I know is what you read too. He hasn't called me, and I haven't been able to reach him. I think he's an honest man, but you don't always know people as well as you think." To both of them, this seemed huge and frightening if the accusations were true and he was in as much trouble as they said. "I'll let you know as soon as I hear something. There has to be an

explanation." But she wasn't sure, and doubt and fear were gnaw-
ing at her.

"I hope so, Mom," Aden said, worried for her too, on the chance
that she could somehow be implicated also because of her close
association with him. It had crossed Maggie's mind as well. She
didn't know what to think.

Late that night, she finally heard from Paul. He sounded tired
but calm. There was no panic in his voice and he apologized pro-
fusely for not calling her for nearly four days.

"I've been on the phone constantly with lawyers in four countries, and tax authorities here in the U.K. and in the U.S. Bottom
line, they don't like my corporate setups, but I've always been
careful to stay just this side of the line. What we've done isn't illegal, but undeniably we've kept my money out of the hands of the
tax guys in both countries whenever we could. We knew it might
come to this one day, but it's been worth it. And we've known there
was something brewing for the last three or four weeks, but I
didn't want to worry you. We've been creative, but not dishonest.
Tax laws keep changing so it's easy to find yourself on the wrong
side of the line, but we keep a close eye on it. Whenever the laws
changed, we shifted our setup to accommodate them. They're
going to have a hell of a time proving that I did something wrong.
Sometimes how you read the law is a matter of interpretation. It's
not always crystal clear. I've got corporations in Hong Kong, Luxembourg, the Bahamas, the Cayman Islands, Japan, the U.K., and
the U.S. We knew that they'd object to Luxembourg eventually,
and they don't like the Cayman Islands, but I pay hefty taxes in the

States. In the end, after they try to shake me up for a while, it'll come to a negotiation about how much I'll pay, but they have to make a lot of noise first to scare me. I'll lose some money on this, but hopefully not too much. And it has saved me a lot till now. I know it sounds bad, but I'm not worried. I took the risk that part of the roof might fall in one day, but not the whole house. I'll probably have to repatriate a nice chunk of change back to the U.S., which is infuriating, but just the way it is. Most of my investments are still safe offshore and will stay that way, owned by sheltered corporations they can't invade. I've been protecting myself for a long time, and they know it. They hate that. I have money in Malta too, which the Brits and the U.S. can't touch."

"It sounds like a lot of work keeping it all straight," Maggie said softly. She didn't like his operating so close to the line of the law.

"It is a lot of work, but it's worth it. I've been lucky. I've made a lot of money and invested it well. I'm not going to give that up if I don't have to. What I've done is legal, it's just complicated to put it in place, and I spent a lot of money doing it. I have an Irish passport too, which was useful at one point, but less so now, since they changed the laws on that again."

He sounded amazingly calm as he explained it to her. It was so typical of him to take an enormous risk, no matter what the consequences later on. He dealt with it when it happened, like his racing suit on fire when he crashed. He put the flames out then, and was willing to total the car to win the race. But who was winning this time? The IRS or Paul? She couldn't tell.

"Could you go to jail for it?" she asked him.

"I might, but that's highly unlikely. I've been incredibly lucky with my investments abroad. They've multiplied exponentially, and if I have to go to jail for a year to save millions, it's worth it. But I can pretty much promise you, it won't come to that. It will all happen in negotiation, and if they have to give me the choice of going to prison instead of paying them, they lose. They won't let that happen, and neither will I. I've already shut down Luxembourg and conceded there, and we'll probably have to shut down some other things, but I've got smart lawyers and most of my holdings are well protected, and technically they're legal, not by a lot, but just this side of the current laws. I'm not dying to go to prison, so we haven't been stupid, just very smart." A little too smart, it sounded like, or the IRS wouldn't be at his throat.

"What about the apartment in London? The article I read said it had been seized."

"True. They put a lock on it and sealed it two days ago, with everything in it. I'll probably have to give that up too. It's just window dressing, and I'd rather give them that than my more serious holdings. I can always buy new clothes. They can't touch the *Lady Luck* or the plane, they're registered offshore and completely protected. If I have to, I can live on the boat. I definitely can't come back to the States now, until this is resolved. I need to stay in the countries that won't extradite me. Possibly France, Switzerland, some others. The Italians will probably turn a blind eye. I'll clear out of London soon, and I can't come to visit you in the States for now, until we make a deal with the IRS." To him, it was just business, to Maggie it sounded terrifying. But he insisted that he had been honest, just smart. And there was a staggering amount of money involved. Maggie couldn't even imagine it. The money she had socked away in conservative investments for Aden's future was peanuts compared to what Paul had amassed and dealt with on a daily basis, but to earn that kind of fortune from his success and preserve it by legally avoiding taxes in some way required enormous risks, which Paul was willing to take. He walked on the edge of the cliff in every area of his life, fearlessly and even foolishly ignoring the abyss. To Maggie, it was a frightening way to live. To Paul, it was a thrill and seemed worth it. He actually enjoyed it, and was willing to take on the IRS.

She was sad for him, thinking of the beautiful penthouse he had just lost in London, but he didn't seem to care. He had his eye on the bigger picture, which was much bigger than a fancy apartment. He made it clear that he had carefully sheltered his boat and plane and most of his investments.

"The *Lady Luck* is under lockdown in Monaco, while they check out the registration and see what they have to do to grab her. But we already know they can't. She's not even registered in my name. She should be in the clear within a few weeks. And the plane too, which is grounded at Gatwick for now. The IRS would like to charge me fines for the way they're registered, but they won't be able to do that either. I was damn sure of that when I set it up. It'll all come right in the end, Maggie, I promise. I have great lawyers. We're already negotiating with the IRS. It's all a chess game." It reminded her of the way he gambled, for enormously high stakes. Nothing seemed to frighten him. He thrived on it. "Don't worry about it." It was easy for him to say, she was worried for him anyway.

"Could the British arrest you and extradite you?" she asked.

"They might. I'm going to Paris in a few days for a while, or skiing in Switzerland until this gets worked out. The French and the Swiss won't extradite me. And none of the European countries put you in jail for taxes, or very few and very rarely. In the U.S., they might, to prove a point. It's really just a dispute about what kind of deductions I have a right to, and what's taxable in the U.S. We have a disagreement about it. They'll settle with us in the end. It'll cost me, but not as much as they want. You have to be smart about taxes, Maggie," he advised her, but it sounded like he had been too clever and too bold, oblivious to the risks, or maybe even excited by them.

"How long do you think it will take to get worked out?" she asked him. This was all new territory to her.

"A few months," he said. "Maybe a year. Two or three at most. I'm not worried about it. A friend is going to lend me his villa in Gstaad, if I want it. I have the suite at the Ritz in Paris, and I'll be on the boat this summer. The only reason for me to come to the States right now is you. And if you're willing, I'd love to see you here in Europe."

She hesitated, thinking about it, wondering if she could get in trouble too, for associating with him. "It's not contagious, I promise." He laughed, guessing what she was thinking. "Come and meet me in Paris. I promise, everything will be fine." She wasn't so sure. This was all so unfamiliar to her, it was overwhelming.

"Where are you staying now?" she asked, shaken by everything she'd heard.

"At my club in London. They're too polite to drag me out in handcuffs, and they have no reason to. I'll go to Paris tomorrow or the day after, before they get too nasty here. I think the British consider it vulgar to go to the lengths I do not to get scalped by taxes. The Americans expect it, but feel it's their job to stop people like me from being smarter than the IRS. It's just business, Maggie, and every man for himself. It's going to be okay. I don't want you to worry about it. Leave it to me, and the lawyers."

"But what if you go to jail?" The thought of it was unimaginable to her.

"I won't. I've been paying enormous amounts to the IRS for years, I'm not some scumbag who's been dodging taxes. They're just pissed that I did such a good job protecting myself, and they want some of what I was able to preserve. We've been very aggressive, and it paid off. So they want part of my winnings, so to speak. It's bad sportsmanship on their part, but it's the nature of the game. They're the big thug who grabs you in the alley and tries to steal what you just won fair and square in the casino. So I'll give them some and they'll be happy, and it'll be business as usual after that. It will all die down. You'll see. It will be a non-event in the end." She wanted to believe him, but felt a million miles out of her league. It was all a game to him. He loved it, especially if he could beat the IRS. He was a very clever man, who hired the right people to help him do what he wanted. And he clearly had no regrets about the problems it was causing him. It was all worth it to him.

In his mind, he was winning the race, again, even if he had lost a fabulous apartment and everything he had in it. To him, that was a detail, compared to the rest. Like damage to a car when he won a race. He expected it.

"I won't let anything happen to you, Maggie. I swear. If I thought you were in any danger, I wouldn't let you come here, and I'd stay away from you until I knew it was safe. This is just a business deal between me and the IRS, a lot of posturing and noise, like what they released in the press. They may have to print retractions later, if they're not careful, but it'll die down eventually. It will boil down to hand-to-hand combat between their experts and mine. I have good people on my team. And I don't intend to lose." He was a formidable opponent, just as he was a legendary race car driver, fearless and brilliantly capable at everything he did. The risk-takers won all the big prizes in the end, or died trying. She knew that too. His was a tough team to be on, and she wasn't sure she was ready for it, or wanted to live with the stress that went with it. She hadn't counted on his playing his life-and-death games with his taxes and the IRS too. There was so much to worry about with him, but he was good to her, she loved him now, and she knew he loved her too. "Will you meet me in Paris?" he asked her gently, and she hesitated.

"Let me think about it."

"Everything will be calm. We can go to Gstaad if you want to get away. We won't be able to use the *Lady Luck* for a few weeks, but she should be released pretty quickly, and everything will be back in order."

"You're a force to be reckoned with, Paul Gilmore," she said with a sigh. "What happened to the boy with the skateboard who raced motorcycles?" He had been scary enough, but the grown-up version was a man of epic proportions, a Mount Everest of men.

"He grew up, got smart, made a lot of money, and learned how to take care of himself."

"And risk his life in every way he could think of."

"I'm not risking my life with the IRS. We're just squabbling over money, like kids playing marbles in the backyard. I told you, this is all a negotiation." She couldn't conceive of how much money was involved, but it was a lot more than marbles. Winning was all that mattered to Paul, no matter what it took or what it cost him. And maybe he would win this time too. She hoped so, for his sake. If he was wrong, and he went to prison, she would be devastated for him, and herself.

She wanted to think again about what she was signing on for, and get some advice from her own lawyer. She had Aden to think about, and couldn't take crazy risks herself. "Take your time," Paul said calmly. "I'll be waiting in Paris when you want to come over. I love you, Maggie. I'm sorry if you got scared by all this bullshit. It's just a lot of noise." He sounded so convincing and she wanted to believe him, but she was scared anyway. It was a long way from her peaceful life with Brad. "Call me whenever you want," he told her. "You'll be able to reach me now."

She hung up, thinking of everything he had told her, it was a lot to absorb at once, and she wanted to believe him, but she wasn't sure she did. She left a message for her lawyer, who called her back in the morning. Maggie told her the whole story, as much as she knew of it. There was always the possibility that Paul hadn't told her everything, or was lying to her. Anything was possible.

Her attorney listened carefully to everything she said, without interrupting, and then said that she didn't know enough about tax laws at that level and referred her to an expert in the field. One consultation with him was going to be very expensive, but Maggie thought it was worth it to assess how much trouble Paul was in. She called the expert and got an appointment for a phone conference with him that afternoon.

Maggie gave him all the details she knew and Carson McGregor listened attentively. He said that he couldn't give her an accurate assessment of Paul's situation without the files, but "rough and dirty," in his experience highfliers like what Paul had become often overshot their reach, intentionally or not. They overestimated what they could get away with, with offshore corporations, properties, and investments, and sooner or later the IRS caught on to them, and went after them to the degree they could. He said the tax laws changed constantly, hoping to catch guys like him. But often men like Paul and their lawyers stayed a step ahead.

"He probably has some very smart attorneys to protect him. It sounds like there's a lot of money involved, and the IRS doesn't give up easily. Is he a gambler?" he asked, curious about him.

"Yes, he is."

"I'm not surprised. He probably expects to win. And he may. It's all a game. He's right about that, and often a negotiation. If the IRS gets riled up enough by his fancy footwork, they may take a big bite out of him, wherever they can get it. But in the end, they'll probably come to terms with him. He knows what he's talking about. It's almost always negotiable, and he and his attorneys are probably good at that."

"Could he go to prison for it?" she asked, worried. She was in love with him, but wanted to steer clear if he was a flat-out criminal, instead of a guy who was too clever, and trying to avoid U.S. taxes to the degree he could. He had obviously stepped over that line, innocently or not.

"Technically, he could go to prison, but I doubt that they'd do that to him. They'd rather negotiate with him to repatriate some of what he has in shelters in offshore tax havens, which he probably won't do if they put him in jail anyway. And he can stay out of the country, in other countries that won't extradite him. There are a number of them. The IRS would probably prefer to play ball with him, if he will, even if they lose some money on it. He's right about that too. He clearly knows what he's doing. This is a major-league game. You have to be very smart and have good nerves for it."

"He doesn't even sound worried."

"Guys like him are willing to take the risk. I couldn't sleep at night if I had the IRS breathing down my neck, but he probably assessed the risk a long time ago, and will push it as far as he can. And they won't go after you, Mrs. Mackenzie, if you're concerned about that. This is all about him. I'm sure your tax records are clean. And you're not married to him. You have no vulnerability."

"My records are squeaky clean," she said, somewhat relieved by what the lawyer said.

"Then you have nothing to worry about," he reassured her. But she was still worried about the mess Paul was in.

She spoke to Aden that night and reassured him. "I've spoken to Paul, my own lawyer, and a tax expert. It's over my head, but apparently this is a battle between Paul and the IRS about how his foreign corporations and investments are set up, and the IRS wanting to discredit some of it to get more taxes from him. Supposedly, it'll wind up a negotiation and some kind of settlement in the end. No one seems to believe he'll go to prison. Paul admits that he and his tax lawyers have been very aggressive about protecting him, too much so, so now they have to justify it to the IRS. He's not upset by it, and said he expected it sooner or later."

"He must be a very smart guy," Aden said, full of admiration for him, which Maggie wasn't thrilled about. Aden hadn't even met him, but was prepared to forgive anything he'd done, and believed that he was right.

"It sounds like a nightmare to me. The British authorities seized his penthouse and it sounds like he's going to lose it."

"Will he lose the boat?" Aden sounded disappointed about that.

"Apparently not. He says it can't be touched. But still, even if he saved a bunch of money on taxes, this isn't an ideal way to do it, not to this extreme." But it was the way he did everything. He was an exciting person, but also a fearless one, which made him dangerous to himself, if nothing else.

"I'm glad he's going to be okay. The article in the *Times* made it sound a lot worse," Aden said, relieved.

"Well, he's not worried, so I wanted to let you know," she said.

"When are you going to see him again?" he asked her.

"I don't know. Maybe soon. In Paris. I'm figuring it out and deciding now." She didn't tell him Paul was going to Paris so he couldn't be extradited to the U.S. and possibly put in jail, even temporarily. She'd never known anyone who had gone to jail for any reason. She knew that as an accountant, and very conservative in his views, Brad would have been horrified by how Paul did business and the risks he took, and would have wanted no part of it. But Brad was part of a different world. Paul lived on top of Mount Everest somewhere, and played life by different rules. Paul was not a criminal, it turned out, if everything he said was true, but he didn't live by the book either, and Maggie always had. Everything about Paul's life was new to her, and so was he. He was no longer the boy she knew at seventeen by any means. She believed him now, but she wasn't sure if she could live that way too, or if she wanted to.

She left for Paris two days after she spoke to Aden about Paul. In the end, she missed Paul, and everything that was happening to him seemed so traumatic to her that she wanted to be with him, even if he claimed he wasn't too upset about it. But he looked tired when she got there, and he was grateful she had come. As always, he made everything perfect for her. He spent as much time with her as he could, between serious business and legal calls from around the world. They went for long walks. He took her to romantic restaurants at night, brought her flowers, told her how much he loved her, and made her laugh. He still behaved like a kid at times, despite the vast amounts of money he moved in international financial circles, and the massively successful, world famous career he had. He had another race coming up in France in May, which she dreaded. But other than the races he still contracted for, his life-threatening career, and the drumroll of the IRS in the background, her life with him actually felt normal most of the time. She wondered if he was crazy, or she was, but they were able to detach from the hard things in his life, and spend time together like any ordinary couple.

He bought bicycles for them, and on weekends they pedaled around the Bois de Boulogne and picnicked in the park, before going back to his luxurious suite at the Ritz. There was a disconnect between the joys and the risks in his life, which somehow made it possible to be happy with him. And their nights together were pure bliss. He was as tender and loving with her as he had been at eighteen when they kissed. And now so much had been added to their lives, both good and bad. But whatever happened, they faced it together.

She spent April in Paris with him, and planned to leave a few days before his race in May, in order to get back to Lake Forest when Aden was due back from school, to begin his summer vacation. In June Aden would take off for his travels around Europe with his friends. Maggie planned to go back to Paul in Europe then, after six weeks at home. As Paul had predicted, the ownership of the *Lady Luck* had been cleared, despite the IRS's best efforts to impound it, so it was back in Paul's control, at the dock in

Monaco, and Maggie was planning to meet him there in June for the summer they had planned. In spite of everything, their life was going smoothly, and it was full steam ahead. Aden could hardly wait to spend July on the boat with them.

At times, Maggie couldn't understand what was happening to her. The life she shared with Paul was one of constant contradictions. Exquisite ups and terrifying downs, blissful nights and the fear that it could all go wrong and the IRS would put him in prison, despite what Paul said. She had the feeling that Paul would always love her, and that he meant all the promises he made her, but it could all end in a burst of flames on the racetrack. Paul was like lightning bolts in the sky, exciting, powerful. He brilliantly lit the darkness around him, but there was no way to predict what he would do next, or what terrifying, breathtaking challenge he would take on. Being with him was dizzying and frightening, but at other times she knew she had never been as happy in her life. It was a roller coaster ride from morning until night, but the best one of her life, and until now, she had never even liked them. And now she didn't want to get off and was hanging on for dear life.

Chapter 12

Although Maggie missed Paul, it felt good to spend six weeks at home in her own bed without him. Aden came home, and she lost herself in the ordinary pursuits of buying groceries and doing his laundry. It was a calming balance to life at the Ritz in Paris, and waiting to see what Paul would do next. Nothing new had emanated from the IRS, and just as he had said, it had become a high-stakes negotiation involving millions of dollars. That in itself had an unreal quality to it, as did life at the Ritz with all the luxuries it offered.

She had made a little progress with the business she wanted to start online, and had contacted a few artists who said they'd be interested in being represented by her. They were young and emerging artists whose work she'd seen at art fairs and galleries in Chicago when she had time, two of the artists were in London and one in Paris. The artists liked the sound of her online concept and the opportunity she was offering them. She wanted to sell the work at moderate prices, which was better than what they were getting now with no permanent gallery. Maggie wasn't ready to set it up yet, but it was much on her mind. She was too busy with Paul to deal with it right now.

Paul had suggested that they could ship works to their clients on approval if the client had proper credit. The idea appealed to her, but the six weeks she spent with Paul in Paris and then the next six weeks spent at home with Aden kept her from making much progress. She was always either busy with Paul, or being available to Aden, which ate up her time.

She talked to Helen about it again when she got back.

"I don't see how you can focus on starting a business, run halfway around the world to be with Paul between his car races and his battle with the IRS, come home to be a suburban mom, and then fly off again. I'm not sure how you're keeping it all straight. Just hearing about it makes me feel crazy. Do you really think his mess with the IRS will turn out okay?" Helen asked her. She and Jeff had discussed it, and it was way over their heads too. It was financial manipulation at the highest level.

"It seems to be under control. I'm more worried about his races again now." His race in France had gone well, he'd come in third, which he wasn't happy about, but at least he hadn't gotten injured. "I feel like a bullfighter's girlfriend," Maggie commented. "I worry about his getting gored every time. It was a lot easier being married to an accountant. My mother was right, the exciting ones will kill you. Especially Paul. The races aren't enough for him, everything he does is dangerous. He's either taking on the IRS, or wants to go skydiving with a friend, or goes mountain climbing to relax. I told him I'd kill him if he does anything dangerous with Aden this summer. He wanted to buy a special boat to take him paragliding behind the *Lady Luck,* and I wouldn't let him. So he bought new high-speed Jet Skis instead. Aden is going to love them. It's fun being with him, but too much fun at times." She had gone from one extreme to the other, and yet there were other times when he was content to share some quiet time with her. They had spent a peaceful weekend in Switzerland before she left, and it was idyllic.

"Let's face it. If you can stand the pace, it beats driving car pool as the high point of your day in Lake Forest," Helen reminded her.

"I'm not so sure." Maggie smiled at her, but she was looking forward to joining him on the boat and having Aden with them, and he could hardly wait.

"We're taking the boys to a dude ranch in Wyoming this summer," Helen told her.

"That sounds great to me." Maggie and Helen had managed to stay in touch and see each other despite Maggie's coming and going and the fancier life she led with Paul now. It hadn't gone to her head, and she appreciated Helen's friendship. She never forgot Helen's getting her moving again after Brad's death, and pushing her to take the trip to Europe, which had changed her life when she reconnected with Paul in Monte Carlo. It was hard to believe it was only nine months ago.

* * *

When Aden left on his backpacking adventure in Europe in June, Paul was already on the boat, working from there by phone and computer. Maggie flew to Nice and joined him on the *Lady Luck* in Monaco. They set sail the night she arrived, and took off for Portofino. As she stood on deck, feeling the wind in her hair, she could feel herself relax. Paul stood next to her with his arm around her. He looked as happy as she did. Everything else faded away when they were together.

"I missed you, Maggie. You were gone for such a long time." He sounded wistful, and she nestled closer to him.

"It was only six weeks." She looked up at him with his blue eyes and gray hair, and had the odd feeling that they had always been destined to be together. They were soul mates, despite how different they were.

"I hate it when you leave," he said softly.

"When you clear things up with the IRS, you can come with me." But she couldn't see him in her suburban life in Lake Forest. Maybe in Chicago or New York. Despite his even more humble beginnings, he had become far more sophisticated than she was. He loved the trappings of his life, and she was happy on the boat with him. When they reached Portofino late that night, after anchoring outside the port, they went for a moonlight swim together. There was a castle lit up far above them, an ancient monastery, and the tiny port looked like a postcard. His crew had floated candles on the water for them, and then left them alone to swim in peace. They took their bathing suits off once they were in the water, and left them on the ladder leading back up to the lower deck. He had a way of making everything seem perfect. He created magic for her.

They swam for a few minutes and then he kissed her, and she dove under the water and swam away from him. He chased her until they both had to come up for air and he kissed her again as their bodies shimmered like ivory just below the surface.

"How did I ever get lucky enough to find you again?" he said, looking at her in wonder as she put her arms around his neck and wrapped herself around him.

"If I hadn't come to Europe, I would never have found you."

"And you'd be leading a peaceful life in Lake Forest without me," he said, kissing her neck, and feeling her breasts against him.

"And bored to death," she admitted. It was the first time she had ever acknowledged it, even to herself. Her life without him would have been fatally dull, which it never was with him. A little too exciting at times, but most of the time, she enjoyed the life she shared with him. The past six months had been some of the happiest of her life. She loved coming home to him. They swam for a little while longer, and then decided to retire to his cabin, which was large and comfortable and beautifully decorated. They laughed trying to struggle back into their wet bathing suits, and laughed harder when they couldn't get into them. Paul managed to put his on inside out, and the bottom of hers had slipped back into the water and disappeared when she left it on the steps. The crew had left towels for them, and she managed to wrap herself in one and get back up the ladder, as they laughed like mischievous children and scampered back to his cabin. Their bathing suits lay in a wet heap on the floor a few minutes later, and they celebrated her homecoming, and then fell asleep in each other's arms, as the boat rocked gently. There was nowhere on earth that Maggie wanted to be, except with Paul.

They took the tender into port the next morning to have coffee in town and explore the shops in Portofino. Paul bought two enormous Super Soakers and an arsenal of water guns and water balloons, while Maggie bought two new bikinis and a pair of sandals.

"What are those for?" she asked him when she saw the bags full of water guns.

"They're for Aden and me," he said proudly. He had bought a pirate flag to go with them, and she laughed at him.

"He's going to love you. I'm not coming out of our cabin with you two on the loose." He showed her the water balloons he had bought too, and she was still laughing at him when they got back into the tender to return to the boat. "How old did you say you are? Twelve?" He had ordered new fishing poles for them too, and was going to take Aden diving. Maggie had said he could, since Aden was certified. It made her think that Paul should have had children of his own. He would have been good with them. She wondered if he should be with a younger woman. It wasn't too late for him, although it felt far too late for her. He had just turned fifty and she was forty-nine. She didn't want another baby, she was happy just being with him. Aden was enough for her, and she didn't want to go through heroics to have another child. She was enjoying their adult life and the freedom that went with it, and Paul was definite about not wanting children and said he never had.

They floated around the coast of Italy for the next week, and then went back to France. He took her to Saint-Tropez, where she had never been. It was still early in the season and already crowded, but the shops and restaurants were fun, then they escaped to the boat anchored outside the port at night. The *Lady Luck* would have been too big for the port, and they liked being farther from the action and the crowds in port anyway. On one of their ventures into town to shop, the paparazzi spotted him and followed them, shooting photographs at close range. Then they followed them in a speedboat when they went back to the *Lady Luck,* and Paul had the crew drop curtains around the dining area on deck so they could eat lunch in peace. Maggie wasn't used to that yet, and the onslaught of photographers had taken her by surprise. They shouted his name from the speedboat alongside, hoping he would appear, but he didn't. He stayed discreetly concealed with her behind the curtains.

"That's so weird," she said, musing about it, "and so invasive."

"You get used to it, after a while." He smiled at her. "Although it feels weird to me too. I'll get the Super Soaker out if they come back." She laughed, and they ate their lunch of langoustine, talking and laughing while they relaxed.

They went to a disco one night, after Maggie said it would be fun to go dancing. He put on a clown nose and a fake mustache as they stepped ashore, "so they wouldn't be recognized," he said, and she laughed even harder at that. But after a few dances at the Caves du Roy, the paparazzi spotted them again, so they fled and took a cab back to the port, where the tender was waiting with two of the crew. They hopped in quickly and took off, and this time the paparazzi didn't have a boat to pursue them. They were back on the *Lady Luck* a few minutes later. Maggie tried the clown nose on when Paul took it out of his pocket, and he took a picture of her that they sent to Aden. He texted back a minute later. "What happened to your nose, Mom? Do you have a cold?" They were excited for him to join them, and he was too.

They spent the next few weeks floating around leisurely, and picked Aden up in Monaco in July, after he'd spent three weeks traveling with his buddies. He was planning to join them again for another two weeks at the beginning of August, and then they were going home and, shortly after, back to college.

Paul had been battling with the IRS for four months by then, but the debacle was far from over. The British tax authorities had declared themselves satisfied after seizing the penthouse and its contents, and had closed their files against him. The IRS was still in the heat of its investigation, but Paul seemed as unconcerned as ever, although every few days Maggie heard him talking to his lawyers. He was remarkably calm about it.

* * *

When Aden arrived, he had flown from Edinburgh, two of Paul's crew members went to pick him up in Nice, and Maggie went with them. She was excited to see him, and Paul said he could hardly wait for him to get to the boat. She had a deep tan and looked rested and healthy. She'd been having a relaxing time with Paul. They'd pulled into port in Monaco from Saint-Tropez the night before, and the crew were busy washing the boat down all morning. Paul had assigned a large cabin to Aden, and Maggie had planned the dinner with the chef for that night with all of Aden's favorites. Paul wanted to take him to the casino afterwards, and then they were going to Jimmy'z to dance if he wanted to. Maggie had brought nicer clothes for him in her suitcase, since he didn't have room for them in his backpack, and she knew he wouldn't bother to bring them if she didn't. She thought he might need some decent clothes on the boat if they went out, as they were planning to that night.

Her face lit up the moment she saw him, and she smiled as he approached. He looked like a kid returning from camp in torn jeans, filthy sneakers that had holes in them, and a shirt advertising a bar in Scotland. His hair was shaggy and his backpack looked like it had been run over by a truck. She was laughing when he got to her in the airport.

"What's so funny?"

"You look about ten years old, and I'm happy to see you." He was about to turn nineteen, but he still seemed like a child to her. He slung an arm over his mother's shoulders, and they walked out of the airport together, after he introduced himself to the two deckhands, who weren't much older than he was. One of them was Scottish, and Aden told him on the way back to Monaco all about what he'd done in Edinburgh.

"Can we pick up some food on the way?" he asked his mother. "I'm starving. I didn't get lunch."

"We'll get you something on the boat," she promised, and he nodded. He'd seen a picture of the *Lady Luck* on the internet, but all he had seen was a big sailboat under sail, he had no concept of the comforts available, the size of the crew, the impeccable service, or the beauty of the boat. He looked thunderstruck when they reached the dock and he saw the graceful lines and the length of the boat. She was well over two hundred feet, and an impressive sight.

"Wow, Mom," he said in a whisper, "I didn't think it was this big." Paul had the entire crew lined up to greet him, in their white uniforms with navy collars and the insignia of the boat, an elegant double "L," embroidered on their collars, and gold epaulets. A well-known Italian designer had made them. There were twenty-four crew members on board. They were an impressive group as they greeted Aden when he came across the passerelle onto the boat. Paul was standing in front of them, smiling. Aden was awe-struck as they shook hands and chatted for a few minutes, and then Paul excused himself, said he had to make a call, and he'd be back in a minute.

Aden glanced around and sat down with his mother in the dining area on deck, as they waited for Paul to come back. Aden was grinning and impressed by the activity around him.

"This is incredible. And he's really a cool guy. I knew he would be." As he said it to his mother, something whizzed just over his head, and Aden ducked as a water balloon exploded and splattered against the mast ten feet away from them. Aden looked up and Paul was grinning from the wheelhouse deck as Aden burst into laughter and stood up, waving at Paul.

"I'll get you for that later," he shouted as another one just missed him, and he scampered up the stairs to where Paul was standing. Paul pointed to a basin full of them, and the two of them threw water balloons at the crew members, who ran away, and lobbed a few onto the dock, narrowly missing visitors to a motor yacht next to them. Then the two of them ducked into the wheelhouse laughing like two naughty kids.

"I got some great guns too," Paul told him, and the two of them went back downstairs to Maggie a few minutes later. There was a plate of sandwiches waiting for Aden on the table, a large pitcher of lemonade, and a plate of homemade cookies that smelled delicious. "We'll go out later, and you can try out the Super Soakers then," Paul promised him, and Aden couldn't stop grinning. He could tell it was going to be a wonderful trip. He spotted the pirate flag a few minutes later as he ate the sandwiches.

One of the stewardesses showed Aden to his cabin after that, and he couldn't believe that either. He looked around the saloon and explored the boat for a few minutes, then half an hour later, they motored out of port and headed toward Saint Jean-Cap-Ferrat to go swimming for the rest of the afternoon. Inevitably, Paul brought out the water guns, and they had a water fight with the crew before they went back to port. Maggie sat just inside the dining area, so she didn't get drenched. And then they all swam again, and decided to stay in the area while they ate dinner, and not to go back to the dock in Monte Carlo until afterwards, since they weren't going to the casino until late. The time on the boat was all about having fun and being spoiled and pampered by the crew. It was a wonderful life, which Maggie had adjusted to quickly.

By the time they sat down to dinner that night, Aden and Paul were fast friends, and he felt as though he'd been there forever. The water fight Paul organized had been great. Aden had talked to several of the crew, who were mostly young and very personable, and very well behaved while on duty. Paul asked Aden questions about his trip, and school, over dinner. Aden shyly asked him about racing. Maggie was surprised how much Aden knew about it, and had obviously studied Paul's history. Paul was touched by that too.

"I understand you're a hockey player," Paul said as they ate the steaks Maggie had ordered for them. The one Aden put away was huge. She knew how much he ate, and it never showed. He was tall and slim with huge shoulders.

"Yeah, I love it," Aden said, "but I don't want to play pro hockey after I graduate. I want to do something else, but I haven't figured out what yet. Maybe sports management, or sportscasting for a network." Maggie was relieved he didn't want to do anything more dangerous. "I want to take flying lessons too," he added. She didn't like hearing that.

"I think you're smart not to want to join the NHL," Paul commented. "You'll end up with no teeth and bad knees by the time you're twenty-five." Aden laughed and agreed with him.

"How did you start racing cars?" he asked Paul.

"I raced motorcycles first, when I knew your mom, when we were in high school. I did it in Mexico for a few years after that, and then I got some lucky breaks and started racing cars. It just happened, and one thing led to another. I won some important races and got the sponsor I still have now. Racing has been good to me. But I just have to warn you, your mom will kill me if you start racing cars," he said half seriously, and Aden laughed.

"I know. She's not so keen on planes either," he said, and they all knew why. "I'd like to try hang gliding. I have some friends who do it in Vermont. It looks cool."

"And dangerous," Paul said. Aden nodded but seemed undaunted.

"Could I go up the mast tomorrow?" Aden asked him. "One of the deckhands said you have a seat that goes to the top."

"You can if your mom says it's okay." He looked at Maggie then. "It's safe. I do it all the time. He can't fall out." She hesitated and then nodded.

After dinner, they motored back into port. They showered and dressed, and after a glass of champagne, which Maggie didn't object to, they headed for the casino, and Aden loved it.

Paul sat down at a blackjack table, with Aden and Maggie standing behind him, and Aden watched avidly. Paul won ten thousand euros in a few minutes, doubled it and then got up before he got too serious about it. He didn't want Maggie to think he was corrupting her son, but Paul could see that Aden was a good boy, bright and full of life and eager to discover the world. He wasn't as wild and fearless as Maggie had said, but he wasn't meek either. He seemed sensible to Paul, and was exactly the kind of son he would have wanted if he had one. He had his mother's integrity and values. He spoke respectfully of his father, and he thoroughly enjoyed being with Paul.

After the casino, they went to the disco, but didn't stay long. Paul quickly spotted several very pretty young hookers, who in turn spotted Aden, and Paul decided not to let things get started, so they left after a short time. It was almost three in the morning by then, and was late enough. He knew the disco would go till five or six A.M. It had been a fun evening for all of them.

The next morning, Aden and Paul were up early, and Maggie had just gotten to the breakfast table when they hoisted Aden smoothly up the mast, and he loved it. When he came down, he said the view was fantastic. They sailed out to swim after that, and Paul and Aden went out on the new Jet Skis, and then went fishing that afternoon.

In the end, Aden stayed almost three weeks and said it was the best time he'd ever had. He hated to leave, and would have stayed, but he didn't want to disappoint his friends, who wanted to finish the trip with him.

They had a massive water war on the last day, with full-on water balloons flying, and all the Super Soakers and water guns that

Paul had bought in use. Everyone got drenched, including the captain and first officer, and even Maggie, and both sides claimed victory.

Aden looked genuinely sad when he had to leave, and he and Paul hugged each other. "Come back soon with your mom," Paul said in a gruff voice. "It's going to be damn dull around here without you. And take care of her when I'm not around. I have a race coming up in September, and she gets mad when I get banged up. You'll have to come see a race sometime, if she'll let you." But he doubted that she would.

"I'd like that," Aden said, and looked like he was about to cry. Maggie hadn't realized how acutely he missed male companionship, and Paul was everyone's dream father, the perfect hero to look up to. They'd played with every toy on the boat, watched movies at night, swam, sailed, fished. Aden had gone parasailing behind the boat and water-skied, and so had Paul. They had had several long talks about Aden's future, and Paul's philosophies about life. Paul told him that he had some regrets about not settling down, but it wasn't in his nature, and he was lucky to have run into Maggie again. A more settled life wasn't a bad thing, if you found the right woman. He hadn't at the right times, and now he was just enjoying his life and playing it out until the end.

"Be careful," Aden had said to him, and they hugged one last time before Aden left the boat and waved from the dock. Maggie rode to the airport with him, and was sad when she came back.

"He loves you," she told Paul in a tender voice. "I mean really loves you. Thank you for being so good to him."

"I love him too. He's a great kid. He misses his dad a lot. I could never take his place. I'm not that kind of guy. You two brought up a wonderful boy and taught him all the right things. But I can be his friend now. I'd be honored to."

"He thinks you're the greatest thing that ever lived." She smiled at him. "And I kind of agree with him," she said and leaned over and kissed him. He pulled her onto his lap and hugged her as they watched the sun set over Monaco. They were setting sail for Corsica that night. He liked sailing at night, and she had come to love it too. They would motor part of the way because it usually got rough in Corsica on the way to Sardinia.

"You're an incredible woman, Maggie," he whispered and then kissed her. "I understand better now why you don't like crazy risks. Aden needs you. And so do I."

"I need you too . . . try to remember that," she said in a serious voice, and he nodded. But he made no promises. He never did. He knew that the forces that drove him were stronger than he was, maybe even stronger than his love for her.

Chapter 13

Maggie left Paul in Monaco in mid-August to fly back to the States and meet Aden at home. He was spending two weeks there before going back to Boston for school. He talked a lot about Paul. The rest of his trip had been anticlimactic after his time on the boat. Nothing measured up to that, but more than the boat, he respected the man. He saw Paul as a brave warrior and a valiant person, who had lived by what he believed in, and had been true to himself all his life. Maggie didn't disagree, but she also saw what it had cost him and that, except for her, he was alone. His skill as a driver was undeniable, and he was said to have the best eye and the best reflexes in racing, and nerves of steel to go with them.

Paul raced in Italy in September, had another lucky race, and won first place this time, uninjured. Every time he finished a race alive, she felt as though he had returned from the dead. She didn't care if he won or lost, she just wanted him to survive it. That was her only prayer for him.

She spent a week in Chicago and a week in New York, visiting galleries, trying to get ideas for the gallery she wanted to open online. She had a list of artists now that she wanted to represent, and little by little she was getting closer. She attended parents' weekend again at BU, and then flew to Paris to meet Paul. His debacle with the IRS still wasn't over, but they were getting closer to a settlement with him. They were going to take a huge financial bite out of him, but no more than he had expected, or was willing to give up. And finally at the end of October, they arrived at a number that satisfied both Paul and the government. He had adjusted his international corporations and investments sufficiently to satisfy them, without crippling himself completely. Both sides had a healthy respect for each other when it was over. He was able to come to the States again without fear of a warrant being issued for his arrest for tax evasion, and Maggie invited him to spend Thanksgiving with them in Lake Forest. He accepted. He and Aden couldn't wait to see each other. Maggie loved the idea of his joining them there at last. He had never seen her home, and she wanted him to, even though it was simple and not as grand as any of his. She wanted him to meet Helen and Jeff, who was dying to meet him. Helen was too, for other reasons, since Maggie had been with him for almost a year by then.

Before they returned to the States, after the settlement with the IRS, they flew to London from Paris, and Paul bought another apartment. It wasn't as grand as the penthouse he had lost, but it was warm and beautifully done, and Maggie loved it. He bought it for her as much as for himself, and there was a suite for Aden that Paul said he would love. He could visit them whenever he wanted to.

Maggie was going to furnish it after the holidays. Paul said he wanted a pied-à-terre in New York too, since he had business there. Maggie thought she would base her online gallery in New York and London, possibly with a rep in each city who could meet with clients to show them art they were considering. She still had some things to figure out, but wanted to open in the new year. She was going to show the work from slides, it was all by emerging artists she had discovered. She was planning to set the prices in the mid to lower price range, to make valid art by talented artists available to collectors who didn't have a fortune to spend on it. She wasn't sure if she'd make money, but she liked the concept of matchmaking new artists with young collectors. She'd have to see how the geography worked. Paul had encouraged her all along and was proud of her for wanting to launch a business of her own, with an original concept. He liked the work she had been considering, and the artists, and had even seen a photo of a piece he wanted to buy from her. And if they had a client in Chicago, Helen was happy to pitch in. Maggie had already registered the name of M. M. Mackenzie for her new business.

After he bought the apartment in London, Paul planned to spend a week there, while Maggie flew home to Lake Forest to get the house ready for Paul and Aden. She'd thought seriously about how strange it would be to share her bedroom with him, but Brad had been gone for two years, and she felt ready to have Paul stay with her there.

The night before she left him in London, Paul reminded her that he was going skiing in Canada right after Thanksgiving. He had mentioned it before in passing, and she hadn't paid close attention. It was a trip he took annually with the same four friends and a guide he met up with once a year, and she frowned when he reminded her. He was planning to leave the day after Thanksgiving, and would be gone a week.

"Why then?" she asked, disappointed that he wouldn't stay through the Thanksgiving weekend.

"It works best for everyone, and our guide."

"Where in Canada?" He hadn't invited her to go with him, and had said that the trip was all men, all expert skiers. It was an arduous trip and they loved it. Two of them had climbed Everest with him, which was how he had met them.

"British Columbia. Revelstoke. We'll take the plane up to Kelowna near Vancouver, and from there we take a helicopter to our ski drop-offs at the Selkirk and Monashee Mountains." The only way into the area was by helicopter. "The lodge is at the base of the mountains. They drop us off on the mountains by helicopter every day, and we ski out. It's rugged terrain but fantastic skiing. The best there is." She was silent for a moment, thinking about it, and looked at him.

"And the most dangerous skiing there is, if I remember correctly."

"It doesn't have to be. We're all good skiers. Our lead guide is a member of the International Federation of Mountain Guides, and we have a tail guide this time too. We carry radios and avalanche equipment. We each wear a transceiver, and carry a shovel and probe. We've got everything we need. Our lead guide knows the area, and the pilot has been doing this for years. This is our tenth year going." She wanted to ask him not to do it, but didn't see how. She couldn't ask him to change all the things he loved about his life, so she said nothing. He saw in her eyes that she was frightened. He held her for a moment and she was stiff in his arms. "It'll be fine, Maggie. I promise."

"You terrify me," she whispered to him. "Why does everything you love have to be dangerous?" It was who he was, and she had known it since he was eighteen, but it didn't make it easier to live with. The more she loved him, the harder it got. Other people died in freak accidents, or on the freeway, in plane crashes like Brad, or had heart attacks when they went jogging, which no one could foresee, but Paul had to put his life on the line at every opportunity, whether playing or racing. He had to steal his life back from the angel of death every time. And what if he lost? She had known it was a possibility since the beginning.

They didn't talk about it again that night, or the next morning, when she took a commercial flight from London to Chicago. There was no point bringing up the ski trip again. It was just something she had to live with, like his racing. His recent win had made him cockier than ever. He needed danger like other people needed air. She thought about it on the flight back to Chicago and tried to make her peace with his helicopter skiing trip with his friends. She felt as though she would be nagging if she brought it up again. He had survived it nine times before this, so presumably he would again. He was a man's man, and she told herself that this was what they did.

She was busy once she got home to Lake Forest. As it always did now, her house felt tired and deserted to her when she saw it again. For the past year she had been commuting to the luxurious spaces in Paul's life, the *Lady Luck,* with its fabulous crew that waited on her hand and foot, the Ritz in Paris and his suite there in the opulence and glamour of the venerable hotel, his penthouse apartment before he lost it to British taxes, the new one he had just bought in a lovely building in one of the best neighborhoods. Coming home to Lake Forest, and their modest home there, was a reminder of the realities of her life, and how she had lived with Brad for nearly twenty years. They had a very comfortable home and she loved it, but she realized now that she had gotten spoiled, and she wondered how it would look to Paul when he saw it.

She tried to spruce it up as best she could, threw away some tired old decorative cushions on the couch, bought new plants and fresh flowers. She tried to fluff things up, and moved a few things around in her bedroom, but the house looked sad now, whatever she did. She realized now how little charm it had, even if they had been happy there. Her life was in a different place now with Paul, and she wondered if it looked shabby to Aden when he came home too, or maybe at his age he didn't notice, and it was just home to him. Without meaning to, they had quietly outgrown it, and it seemed so small to her after the bigger spaces she had gotten used to.

She did her best, and Aden seemed happy to come home. He didn't even see the few improvements she'd made. He liked it the way it was, and never wanted her to change anything in his room.

When Paul arrived, the only thing he saw was her, waiting in the doorway to welcome him to her home. It was a major step for them, and made their relationship seem more real.

Aden took charge of Paul immediately, and drove him to all his old haunts: the pond where he had learned to skate, both his old schools, the main street in town where all the shops were, the grocery store where he and his friends had conned someone into buying them beer when they were sixteen. All the landmarks that were important to him, and Paul loved it. He felt as though he was reliving Aden's childhood with him, which reminded him of a better version of his own, since he didn't have a stable family and Aden did. For a moment, he envied Aden how he had grown up, with a mother and father who loved him and each other, in a safe home where no harm could come to him, going to a normal school where kids grew up and went to college and then married and had kids. Paul hadn't had any of that, had to fend for himself as a kid, without a father, and was on his own as soon as he graduated from high school and headed to Southern California and then Mexico to seek his fate and his fortune. It had turned out all right for him, better than that, but he would never have the happy memories that Aden did and was sharing with him now. Aden had had everything Paul had ever dreamed of and never had. Instead, Paul's whole life had been a search for something he had never found, and it was all here with Maggie and Aden. It made him want to stay here forever with them and try to turn back the clock and start again. He was deeply moved by the tour, and told Maggie that after they got back, when she and Paul were alone. He had tears in his eyes when he told her about it.

"Aden doesn't know how lucky he is," he said softly, as she remembered the terrible shack Paul had lived in, in the town where they grew up, and the mother who had barely managed to make enough to feed him, and the father who abandoned them and disappeared. He had more than made up for it, but he had been struggling all his life, fighting his own demons, battling to stay alive, seeking every challenge, climbing every mountain, winning every race, and he still was. She put her arms around him and he rested his head against her as he basked in the warmth of the love and stability she gave him, which he had never had until then. For an instant, he almost wanted to tell her that he wouldn't go on the ski trip with his friends, but they would think he was an idiot if he did that. All he wanted was to stay there with her. He didn't say anything, but she felt the bond between them without words.

He had arrived three days before Thanksgiving, and she cooked meatloaf for them that night. He loved it. And the following night, they went to the Watsons', so he could meet Helen and Jeff. Jeff monopolized him, but Helen got to see how loving Paul was with Maggie, and she loved him for the way he treated her and the look in Maggie's eyes. Helen thought Maggie was a lucky woman. She had had two men who truly loved her in one lifetime. Some women never had even one. She and Jeff had had their ups and downs, and had finally accepted that it would never be exactly what either of them wanted, but it was good enough. But what Paul and Maggie shared was very different. They were like soul mates who had found each other at last, or found each other again. Helen didn't even think Maggie had been as well suited to Brad, but would never have said it to her, out of respect for the dead. Paul was what every woman dreamed of, and only a rare few ever found. Maggie had.

"If you don't marry him, I will," Helen whispered to her, and Maggie laughed.

"He hasn't asked," Maggie reminded her. In fact, the subject had never come up, and Maggie hadn't been longing to marry him, she was comfortable as she was. They had everything they wanted and needed, and she wasn't sure if marriage was necessary, or if she even wanted it. If she married him, she might wind up a widow again. Although if he was killed racing, married or not, it would be just as bad. "I thought I'd let him calm down a bit, before I think about it. Like maybe when he's eighty or ninety. I don't think he'll be civilized much before that. He needs to burn off some energy first. He's going helicopter skiing the day after Thanksgiving. He's officially crazy." Jeff overheard her say it and questioned Paul about it, who said he'd been doing it for ten years.

"I'm the old man in the group now, but they let me come anyway. I figure I'll stop doing it next year. I just turned fifty, so I'm going to make this the last time."

"I've always wanted to do that. Helen won't let me." Jeff cast a glance at his wife and rolled his eyes.

"No problem. Just leave me the full amount for the boys' college education in an account, and you can go helicopter skiing anytime you want," Helen said tartly. "But you're not leaving me stuck with that." They all laughed, but Helen looked serious. Having three kids had been a stretch for them financially, even though Jeff had a good job. She'd given up her own job as a copywriter in advertising to raise them, and it hadn't been easy for them with only one income.

Aden, Maggie, and Paul had dinner in town the next night, and then Aden went out with his friends. The next day they had what Paul called a Norman Rockwell Thanksgiving.

"I used to see pictures in magazines of people who had Thanksgivings like this. I've never seen one for real, let alone had one." He looked on the verge of tears again.

The turkey was a perfect golden brown, the vegetables looked like an artist had painted them. Maggie had set the table with her mother's best lace tablecloth. She had used the china that had belonged to Brad's parents, and the crystal they had bought to go with it. The food was perfect and smelled delicious. Aden sliced the turkey the way he had seen his father do every year, and Paul opened the bottle of wine Aden had taken him to buy the day before. The food tasted as good as it appeared, and for dessert Maggie had outdone herself with apple, pumpkin, mince, and pecan pies, with whipped cream and vanilla ice cream. It was a feast, and their conversation was lively and happy. Aden put music on and they danced afterwards, the three of them, and then he went out with friends, while Maggie and Paul tidied up the kitchen, and then danced to the music still playing. There was an old song from the forties playing that Maggie had always liked, and remembered her mother singing.

"If I die this minute, I'll have been a happy man," Paul whispered to her, and she smiled.

"I'm happy too. I love having you here. I was afraid the house wasn't nice enough for you. You're used to such fancy places now."

"Don't forget where I grew up," he reminded her. "I always dreamed of having a house like this. What I have now is an accident. It's a winning lottery ticket and I know it. This is what I always wanted, and never had. It's my dream. I love this house, and you in it, and Aden and all the places he showed me when I got here: his school, the pond, all of it." It was why she had married Brad, to have a life like this. Paul understood that now and she'd been right. They hadn't needed anything more than this. No one did, in his opinion. This was what made people strong and healthy, and not chasing rainbows all their life. This was the rainbow and the pot of gold at the end of it. It was what most people ran after and never found. He never had. He had found untold wealth from his fame, his investments, and the risks he took, but he had never found this kind of solid foundation, and knew he never would without Maggie. She knew that about him too. He needed her for this. He would never find it on his own. And she hoped that with enough of this kind of love, he wouldn't need to chase the lightning flashes anymore, or the dangers that fell from the sky. He didn't need to climb Everest. All he needed to do was come home, if he could ever figure that out. She hoped he would one day.

They sat in front of the fire for a while, and then they went upstairs and made love. She couldn't feel Brad's spirit in her bedroom anymore. He had been laid to rest. The room was hers and she shared it with Paul with an open heart. His bag was already packed to leave the next day. He fell asleep as she smiled down at him and stroked his hair like a little boy. She held him for a long time, and then went to sleep next to him.

He was leaving at four A.M. to drive his rented car back to Chicago and catch his plane to meet his friends. He was picking them up at two stops along the way and heading north for their big adventure. When he got up, he didn't want to leave Maggie and wished he could stay. It was warm and cozy next to her in bed. It took all the effort he could muster to get up and leave her.

She walked him downstairs in her nightgown, after Paul was dressed. She gave him coffee in a thermos to take with him, and stood in the freezing air in the doorway kissing him. There was ice on the ground outside.

"Go back in, you'll catch pneumonia," he whispered to her. He didn't want to wake Aden, and had said goodbye to him before he went out the night before. Paul was coming back to spend Christmas with them, which was only a month away.

Maggie was staying in Lake Forest for December. The second anniversary of Brad's death would be before she saw Paul again, and she needed to go through it alone. Aden's school vacation started that day, and he was coming home, so they'd be together.

She kissed Paul one last time, and waved as he ran to his car, turned the key in the ignition, and started it. A minute later he took off, with a wave to her. She walked back into the house, shivering, thinking of him. It had been a beautiful Thanksgiving, she was glad he had come. He felt like part of the family now. She knew Paul felt it too. And she knew it was true when Paul had told her it was the best Thanksgiving of his life. It was the best gift she could have given him. Their first Thanksgiving was a memory she would never forget.

Chapter 14

Maggie couldn't get back to sleep once Paul left the morning after Thanksgiving. She felt anxious about the ski trip, and knew she was foolish to worry. Paul was the oldest man in the group, but he was an outstanding skier, probably better than the rest of them. He and the others had been training for several months and were in perfect shape. They had one of the best guides in the business, a superb pilot, and the best equipment money could buy. They knew the area, and had been there before, although they moved around a lot, depending on the snow and weather conditions, so each trip was different from the one before. Paul was in great condition, and kept his body toned and strong. He had climbed Everest, and this was a piece of cake compared to that. Paul had said so. But Everest was sixteen years before, at thirty-four, and this was dangerous enough.

Paul had given Maggie a number she could call to get periodic reports. It was the helicopter dispatch office. She couldn't call Paul directly. There was no cell service where they were staying. They would be carrying radios to communicate with the base and each other, and they were each wearing an avalanche signal, in case they got buried, so someone could find them. They had the most modern equipment for this kind of skiing, and state-of-the-art clothing to keep them warm in the coldest conditions. Paul liked testing his endurance every year, to check how strong he was and how much resilience he still had. There was a tremendous sense of personal accomplishment when he came home after a week of pushing himself that hard. Every year he felt healthy and powerful for months afterwards. It was a rite of passage, a test of one's manhood, which was hard for Maggie to understand. To her it just seemed unnecessarily dangerous, like everything else he did. Paul challenged himself every day, in one way or another. It was his way of proving to himself that he was still alive and at the top of his game. She understood that about him, and the reasons for it, but she wished there were some other way for him to prove himself, without risking his life. She had never understood male rituals like running with the bulls in Pamplona, where office workers and young boys risked getting gored by a bull in the streets of Spain. All a person had to do there was be able to leap over a fence in time. Paul would have to use his utmost skill skiing, and jumping out of the helicopter in just the right way at the right time. He would have to be able to stay ahead of potentially lethal weather conditions, endure the freezing cold, and flawlessly judge the terrain he would be skiing. A single mistake or careless moment could cost him his life, and those of his companions. It was a gamble of the most extreme kind, and precisely what Paul loved above all else. He needed to challenge himself and come home victorious. And she was left to wait it out day by day.

She stayed busy for the first few days. Aden left on Sunday to go back to Boston. She hadn't heard anything by then and didn't expect to. No one was supposed to call her. She could call the helicopter dispatcher if she wanted news of them, but she didn't want to make a nuisance of herself. She thought of calling them on Monday, but decided not to. She did research for her online gallery to keep busy. She still had a lot to do before she could get started.

On Tuesday morning, she turned the TV on in her kitchen while she made coffee, just to hear some friendly voices in the quiet house. She didn't pay much attention to who was being interviewed, and then saw a news bulletin roll across the screen, so she switched to the news channel. They said there had been an avalanche in Western Canada, in British Columbia, the day before, one of the worst in its history. Two groups of expert skiers who had been helicoptered in had disappeared. They had been missing for almost twenty-four hours by then. Maggie could feel her throat get tight as she listened. She could hardly breathe.

She fumbled in her purse for the number Paul had given her, and she called immediately with shaking hands. The dispatcher confirmed that Paul's group was one of the two groups that were missing. They were in fact wearing avalanche transceivers, but a storm had come in, and rescue helicopters had been unable to get into the area. They were waiting for conditions to clear. Maggie could barely formulate the questions she wanted to ask them. She wanted to know how long they could survive in the freezing conditions until they were rescued, but she didn't have the guts to ask them. One day? Two? Four? Five? Ten? None? And how soon did they think the helicopters could go in?

They told her they were hopeful that in the next few hours they could fly a mission, but they might have to wait another twenty-four hours. Another storm front was moving into the area. They gave it to her straight, with no apology and no hesitation. They knew that anyone who skied with them was fully aware of what the risks were. Paul had known them too. It was part of the thrill for him.

"We've had some really nasty weather," the dispatcher told her. "They may all be fine, and we're just too far away to pick up their transceiver signals. We need to get in and be a lot closer. They know what to do. There are no novices in the group. And they've got the best lead guide in Western Canada." But Maggie knew, as he did, that sometimes the experts and the best guides died too. He suggested that she call again that evening, and when she did, he had no news then either. The predicted storm had come in, and all their helicopters were grounded. The rescue patrols had been alerted, but there was nothing they could do. "The weather dictates what we do up here," he said, and Maggie thanked him.

Helen was sitting in her kitchen with her by then, and had been there since Maggie called her in a panic that morning and told her what had happened. Maggie hated to do it, but she had called Aden too. She didn't want him to see it on the news. He sounded devastated when she told him, and he had stayed home from class all day to watch CNN in case there was any news.

"When he comes back, I'm going to kill him for doing this to my kid," she said to Helen through clenched teeth. Aden had nearly burst into tears when she told him.

"Never mind Aden," Helen said, "he's doing this to you too. This is why I won't let Jeff go up there. He thinks he's such a hotshot skier, and he's never climbed Everest like Paul."

"That was sixteen years ago, he's fifty now. He's too old for this and he knows it. He said this was going to be his last year."

Helen refused to leave Maggie alone that night and stayed with her. Jeff felt terrible about what was happening and said he'd stay with the kids. Maggie called Aden again that night, but there was no further news. And it was worse the next morning, on Wednesday. The dispatcher told her they had confirmed reports of a second avalanche in the area during the night. But at least the sky had cleared enough for the helicopter rescue patrols to go in and cruise around, searching for signals.

Maggie reported back to Helen, and they spent another day in her kitchen, watching the news channel, waiting to hear something and periodically calling the dispatcher. Maggie had insisted that Aden go back to class. She didn't want him sitting there, agonized the way they were. She promised to call him as soon as they heard anything. Paul's group had been missing for forty-eight hours by then. It felt like a year. She remembered his stories about Everest and wondered if it had been anything like this.

It was another endless night waiting to hear something, and

Helen had to go home to her kids. She was back at eight the next morning, after her boys left for school. It was Thursday by then, and by noon the other group had been found. Four of them were dead. Two had died of asphyxiation in the avalanche, two had died of broken necks, and the other two had been airlifted out and were in critical condition. There was still no sign of Paul's group. The patrols had hovered over the entire area for as long as they could, and had picked up no signals from their transceivers. There was no evidence of them anywhere. The patrols had questioned if they may have moved faster than expected and left the area, but there was no sign of them in a wide radius. It was almost like searching for survivors at sea.

That night was even harder for Maggie, alone again. She felt like she was reliving Brad's death. All her old signs of PTSD returned and she tried to ignore them. But there was no way she could justify this to herself. He hadn't died in the line of duty for his country like her brother in Iraq, even though that had seemed senseless to her too. He hadn't died while doing his job, like her father. He had done this for sport and to prove something no one cared about, about how big a man he was, and now they couldn't goddamn find him under the snow, and he had probably suffocated or died of a broken neck like the other men. And for what? The full force of what it meant being with him hit her like a wrecking ball while she waited.

The search continued on Friday morning, and the dispatcher told her they were "still guardedly hopeful," which didn't sound good to her. Helen suspected Paul was dead by then, but didn't say anything to Maggie. She felt desperately sorry for her, and Jeff did too.

The patrols found a single signal at noon. Paul's group had been missing for four days by then, and had gone farther afield than the rescue patrols thought they could, possibly trying to avoid the storm that was coming in. There was only one signal, and Maggie selfishly prayed it would be Paul's. They had found each other again after thirty years, and she didn't want it to end like this, with him dead under an avalanche on some kind of insane macho pleasure trip. The rescuers located the other signals that afternoon, scattered in the area. At first they thought there was too much wind to go in. And then, mercifully, the wind died down, and they were able to fly in.

They found Paul's group just before dark. Maggie felt like she was in a daze by then, as she listened to what they could tell her on the phone. Three of the men were dead, the tail guide too. Two were in critical condition. The lead guide was in a coma with a shattered spine. An hour later she learned that Paul was one of the men in critical condition. They were airlifting them to the Trauma Center at Vancouver General Hospital, but by the time they got there, the lead guide had died. He was thirty-six years old and had four kids.

Maggie sat in her kitchen feeling paralyzed, not sure what to do, if she should make a run for it and go to him, or wait for further news once he got to the hospital. He might even be dead by then. She called Aden to tell him Paul was alive but in critical condition. It was all she knew, she didn't know the extent of his injuries, or what his chances for survival were. Probably very slim by now. They had been out there for too long.

"He's tough, Mom, he'll make it," Aden said, wanting it to be true. After she hung up, she knew she wanted to see Paul, before he died, to say goodbye and tell him she loved him. She hadn't had the chance to say goodbye to Brad. Maybe this time she would.

She ran upstairs and threw some things in a bag, toothbrush, toothpaste, underwear, sweaters, jeans. She called the airline, and then Helen to tell her what she was going to do. She called a cab, closed the house, and was at the airport in time to catch a flight to Vancouver. She texted Aden that she was on her way and would call him with any news. It had been a hellish week, worse than anything she had ever been through, hoping he would make it, and terrified he was already dead. She had been afraid they might not even find his frozen body until spring.

She sat rigid in her seat on the four-hour flight, bracing herself to see him. She had no idea what he'd look like after being buried in the snow or exposed to the elements for four days.

When they landed, she took a cab to the hospital, and was told that Paul was in the Trauma ICU when she got there. Without even thinking, she said she was his wife, and a nurse led her in to see him. If she hadn't known it was Paul, she wouldn't have recognized him. His skin was gray with red, burned patches on it, his lips were translucent, and he looked as though he had aged twenty years since she'd seen him.

They were trying to bring his body temperature back up to normal. His hands and feet were frozen and the doctors were watching them closely for signs of frostbite and gangrene. They warned her in the hallway that he might lose his hands and feet. She prayed for him that it wouldn't happen. It would kill him. But even if it did, she suspected he would find a way to do something dangerous and risk his life again. They would have to cut off his head or cut him in half to stop him.

He opened his eyes for an instant and looked as though he recognized her, but she wasn't sure. He blinked but couldn't speak. He didn't have the strength to move, and after he saw her, he sighed and closed his eyes. She thought he had died, but the monitor showed that he was still breathing. She sat next to him while he slept and willed him to live. Two days later, he opened his eyes and spoke to her in a croak.

"Love you . . ." was all he said, and went back to sleep, as tears ran down her cheeks. He was still in critical condition, and all she could do was pray that his ninth life hadn't run out. She sat beside him day and night, and slept on a cot next to him, and the following day he spoke to her in a whisper.

"Last time," he said, and she nodded.

"I'll kill you if you do this again," she whispered back, and he smiled through his badly cracked lips. "I think this was your ninth life." He nodded and when he could speak more clearly, he told her that he had thought of her constantly and it had kept him alive for the four days they were lost. He knew it was the last time for him. She had changed everything. He knew she loved him, and he loved her. He hadn't had children so he could be free to do what he wanted, but now he had Maggie, and he knew when he saw her face that he couldn't do this to her again. She looked ravaged.

"Last time," he said again.

She called Aden and told him how Paul was doing. After a week they took him off the critical list, and miraculously his hands and feet had thawed out and had blood flow again. He wasn't going to lose them unless complications set in.

He had told her that half of his group had been able to dig out with their avalanche tools. The others were already dead by then. The survivors had taken refuge as best they could, huddled together, but couldn't have held out much longer. Surviving four days had been a miracle.

They released him from the hospital after the second week. They had her walk him slowly down the halls, using canes to get him moving again. The toll on his body had been brutal, but he was recovering. They said it was incredible he had survived, and she thought so too.

The *Lady Luck* was on her way to the Caribbean when Paul was ready to leave the hospital, and Maggie told him what they were going to do. She didn't ask him what he wanted, and he didn't argue with her.

"I'm taking you home to Lake Forest to take care of you," she said, and he smiled at her.

"That sounds perfect to me."

"And I'm tying you to the bed if you try to go anywhere," she warned him Aden was coming home and he could help her take care of him, if Paul needed help getting to the shower, or was unsteady on his feet. He was still having trouble walking, but getting better rapidly. He said his feet still felt like blocks of wood or bricks, and the doctors said it would take a while for them to move normally again.

When the hospital released him, he had his plane pick them up and fly them to Chicago, and a car and driver take them back to Lake Forest. The driver helped Maggie get him inside and up the stairs when they got to her house, and Paul looked like he had gone to heaven when he got there. He stopped for a moment before heading up the stairs and gazed at Maggie.

"I kept thinking of you here. I never thought I'd see you or this house or Aden again."

"Neither did I," she said softly. It really was a miracle that he had survived, more than she had dared to hope for, after two avalanches and four days in the freezing snow.

He walked up to her bedroom then, with the limo driver behind him to make sure he didn't fall. Maggie thanked the driver, and after he left, she put Paul to bed, and he sank into the pillows like a man who knew he had no right to be alive but was grateful he was. He glanced around the room. She had already realized that Brad's second anniversary date had come and gone while she was nursing Paul, and she had a feeling he wouldn't mind. He had always wanted her to be happy. She would always love him, and still did, but she knew that this was where she was meant to be now. For some reason, Paul had come back to her, and he had survived the impossible. She knew that her place was with him, and so did he.

"Try to sleep for a while," she said gently.

"Sit next to me." He still looked like an old man and some of the burns on his face were still bright red, but he looked more like himself again, just older.

She sat next to him until he fell asleep, and then she tiptoed out of the room to put some of her things away and tidy up the house. She had left it a mess when she ran out to fly to him. She stood, gazing out the window, and smiled. The man with nine lives had come back to her. It was going to be a very good Christmas after all, for all three of them.

Chapter 15

Maggie took care of Paul on her own for the first few days. She stood in the shower with him to make sure he didn't fall, and gently bathed his burns and injuries. She massaged his hands and feet as the nurses had shown her how to, and soon he was walking almost normally.

Jeff and Helen came to visit him, and gave him a hero's welcome, and Paul and Aden both cried when Aden came home. Aden helped Paul to the shower and down the stairs, and drove him into town so he could buy a few things. Paul told Aden what it had been like, buried, thinking about both of them. He admitted that it had been a foolish thing to do and he wouldn't do it again.

One night while Paul was sleeping, Aden and Maggie decorated the house with the colored lights as they always did. Paul had tears in his eyes when he woke up in the night, and saw it from the window. The next day, he watched them decorate the Christmas tree.

He told her he'd never had one as a boy. He felt like an orphan who had been deposited in a family, and he couldn't believe how lucky he was to be alive and there with them.

Maggie prepared their traditional Christmas dinner, and for the rest of the week, Paul and Aden watched sports on TV, when Aden wasn't out with his friends. Maggie played Christmas carols. Paul wanted to go out, but the streets were icy, and she was afraid he'd fall. He let her keep him home and enjoyed it.

Aden left on the morning of New Year's Eve, to go skiing in Vermont as he had the year before. Paul looked at her after he left. The house seemed empty without him. Paul seemed more like himself again. It had been a month since they found him, and he felt ready to reenter his world. Being in Lake Forest with Maggie was like being in a cocoon. He was ready to spread his wings and fly. She could see that he was getting restless.

"What do you say we get out of here for a few weeks, and spend some time on the *Lady Luck*?" Paul suggested. "She's sitting there in Antigua, and the crew has nothing to do. I could use some warm weather." And they had told him that swimming would be good for his feet. They were almost back to normal, but he hadn't regained full feeling yet, and he knew he needed to. He wanted to get back in shape.

"Do you feel up to the trip?" she asked him, and he laughed.

"I may look a hundred years old, but I'm not a hundred yet." He called the captain and his pilot and arranged for them to be picked up the next day. All he had to do was grab a phone and make magic happen. He had been helpless for the last month, but he no longer was. He was like a sleeping lion coming awake. "I can't believe what good care you've taken of me, Maggie," he said, and kissed her as they lay in her bed that night. She had cared for him like a baby, and nursed him back to life. It was a cozy way to spend New Year's Eve, and she didn't mind. On the boat, he would have his crew to help him. He was getting antsy about his business dealings. His whole life had been on hold for a month, and he had been entirely hers. She had loved it, but knew it couldn't last forever. Sooner or later, he'd be back in the world.

"Happy new year, Maggie," he said to her as he held her, and she smiled up at him.

"Happy new year, Paul. Welcome back."

The next morning, a car arrived to drive them to the airport. Maggie had packed what she needed that morning, and Paul had almost nothing to pack. He'd bought some jeans and slacks and sweaters in the shops in Lake Forest. He decided to leave them there, since he didn't need winter clothes on the boat.

"Take something for New York," he told her as she packed. "I need to spend a couple of days there, after the boat. And then I have to go to London for meetings, and you have an apartment to decorate." That all seemed so far away now, and she was sorry to leave their simple life at her house. But he had things to do, worlds to conquer, and deals to make. She was free again until Aden came home in March, and maybe he'd meet them in Europe for spring break instead. Her life wasn't really here anymore, except for special times like Thanksgiving and Christmas. She had to follow Paul back into his life now. She wondered how quickly it would change after his near-death experience. It wasn't going to leave him where it found him, and he had told her in the hospital that it was "the last time" he risked his life. He had had a transformation while waiting to die for four days. She could see the change. He seemed to savor every moment like a precious gift.

He had sent a large donation to the family of the lead guide who had died, leaving four kids. He'd written a letter of sympathy to the widow. And she had responded stunned and grateful for his generosity.

Maggie wondered when they'd come back to Lake Forest. It didn't sound like it would be soon. She called Helen to say goodbye. Helen raced over before they left to give Maggie a hug and wish Paul luck. And he hugged her back. He liked her, and Jeff, and he knew how important Helen was to Maggie. Maggie had told him how Helen had saved her life after Brad. Now Maggie had saved his. He would never forget it, and treated her with new gratitude and respect as they rode to the airport and got on his plane. He heaved a sigh of relief as he entered his familiar world and felt back in control again. He walked up the steps normally, and walked down the aisle with ease.

"How do you feel?" Maggie asked him on the trip.

"I feel great," he said, roaring like a lion, and she laughed.

"I think my nursing days are over," she said with a touch of nostalgia.

"You sound sorry," he teased her.

"Maybe I am. You're a lot easier to keep track of when you're half frozen and can't walk."

"I'll keep that in mind." He smiled at her. And when they got to the boat in Antigua, the entire crew had lined up on deck to greet him, in dress uniforms, many with tears in their eyes. Once they heard the full story, they couldn't believe he had survived, and neither could he.

"More like ninety-nine lives than nine," the captain said when they talked about it. Paul had the steward serve them all a glass of champagne, and then he and Maggie settled into their cabin. He had asked for a massage and urged Maggie to get one.

"You deserve it more than I do." He wanted her to be pampered to repay her for what she'd done for him. It was the least he could do. He hadn't even been able to get her a decent Christmas present, since he could barely walk then and was still very stiff. He intended to make up for it when they got to New York, and he had something special in mind. She had bought him a cashmere and silk robe, which he had worn constantly and left in Lake Forest for when he went back.

He improved dramatically once he was on the boat. They swam morning and afternoon, the massages brought his feet back to normal, and his hands. Two weeks after they'd arrived, he felt entirely like himself. It was six weeks after his dramatic rescue. He had no traces left of his days buried in the snow after the avalanche, except a few barely pink patches on his face that were rapidly fading, and nothing else. Maggie still looked tired and worried at times. She still had headaches, but didn't tell him. She knew why. The terror of losing him had brought the PTSD back with a vengeance, but it was slowly fading now. The boat was good for her too.

Their plan was to stay on the boat for most of the month. Paul was working at getting back in shape again, and she could tell he was getting strong. He worked out in the gym every day. No one would have guessed what he'd been through. It all seemed like a bad dream now. As she watched him stride across the deck or dive into the water, he looked like the old Paul, or the Paul before Canada. There was nothing old about him now. He looked young and strong again, and not even fifty. She was still quiet but seemed peaceful, and she kept her eye on him for any sign of a problem, but there were none. He had escaped unscathed, again. She hoped he remembered the lesson in spite of it, and his promise to her that it was the last time he would risk his life again.

After the boat, they were going to spend two days in New York. Paul had meetings with his tax lawyers, and wanted to make sure that the changes they had implemented were on track. They had been through that too, and come out of it.

After New York, he said he had to get back to London for serious business, and then meetings in Zurich. "I've got to work all of February, Maggie. I have a lot to catch up on. I feel like Rip Van Winkle waking up." She smiled when he said it. He was already working by phone from the boat for several hours a day. "And I have a race at the end of the month." He said it as though it was an ordinary occurrence, and she stared at him, too shocked to speak for a minute.

"You *what*?" She thought she must have heard wrong. It couldn't be.

"In Spain, at the end of February. And one in Italy in March."

"Are you serious? You nearly died six weeks ago."

"I have a contract, Maggie. I've got two races left before we re-negotiate. They'll sue the hell out of me if I don't honor it."

"Almost dying isn't a valid reason to let you off the hook?"

"There are millions of dollars involved. You know that. And I have no excuse. It was an accident. I've been through worse driving. And I'm perfectly healthy now. I can't drop out of the races. My sponsors would kill me."

"I thought we agreed that you'd used up your ninth life."

"I may have. But I have contractual commitments. I meant it was the last time I'd go helicopter skiing. I'm done with that. But I can't retire yet." And he didn't want to. It was his life, but so was she.

"And the racing?"

"It's my job," he said calmly.

"It's your drug. Risking your life, tempting fate, taunting death. How often are you going to do that?"

"I don't know," he said, looking uncomfortable. "All I know is that right now, I have a contract with two races left. Fortunately, I got hit by the avalanche when I didn't have a race scheduled," he said with a touch of irony, but she didn't smile. He was still Paul. She should have known, but she had believed him.

She didn't argue with him. She knew there was no point. It was crystal clear to her now. There was always going to be one more race, one more ski trip, one more adventure, one more mountain to climb, one more harrowing, death-defying experience while he beat the odds. And one day, he wouldn't win. She didn't want to be there to see it. Her mother had been right about him at eighteen. Brad had been her safe haven for nearly twenty years, and Paul never would be. He didn't have it in him. He needed danger the way other people needed air.

He had a conference call then, and she went to their cabin and looked in the mirror, and saw who she would become if she stayed with him. She would become her mother, broken and sad and depressed and half crazy until she gave in to dementia because she couldn't face reality anymore.

She went swimming alone after that, off the boat, and sliced through the clear water. He was a lucky man, and he didn't even know it. He didn't see what he had, the beauty around him, the people who loved him. All he saw were the risks he had to take, the odds he had to beat, the gambles he had to win. He was a gambler to the core. Since she'd been with him, he'd been injured in a race, risked prison, and nearly died in Canada. It was enough.

She didn't know how she'd explain it to Aden, but she'd find a way. She had buried one man she loved, but couldn't bury two. She'd thought she'd have to after Canada, and somehow he had been spared. Now he was going to risk everything on another race. It had nothing to do with his contract and he knew it too. It was all about him and the demon inside him that needed to dance with death again. And one day, the demon would win.

Chapter 16

Maggie was quiet for the last two weeks on the boat. She rested and swam, and made notes for her online gallery that she knew she had put off for too long, while she focused all her energy on Paul and lived on his schedule.

She didn't mention the race again and neither did Paul. He had told her. That was enough. She didn't need to know more. She didn't need to go anywhere, or argue with him, or try to reason with him. She turned inward, and Paul eventually noticed how quiet she was.

"Are you okay?" he asked, concerned. He thought she seemed tired and pale. She almost looked worse than he did after his near-death experience. After nearly two months of rest, he looked even better than before, and was in flawless shape. He was working out in the gym every day, to get ready to race again, and his hands and feet were fine. The circulation was fully restored. His trainer told him he was a miracle and he knew it too. Maggie had been part of it. She had brought him back from the dead, and he was grateful to her.

"I'm fine," she said softly. She seemed oddly removed to him, and he wondered if she should see a doctor in London or New York. He knew that what had happened to him had been traumatic for her too, and she had been selfless in caring for him. The days in Lake Forest had been among the most tender in his life. No woman he had ever known would have done that for him, but now he was back to life. He had mountains to climb and battles to fight. He had thought of retiring, when he was in the hospital, but knew it wasn't time. If he had lost his hands and feet he would have had no choice. But the way had opened up for him, and he knew that it meant he wasn't ready to quit. He still had races to win. Soon he would be too old, but not yet. He was going to squeeze the last drop out of the fruit that still tasted so sweet to him. He had worried about Maggie's reaction, when he finally told her about the race, but she had taken it well. She hadn't begged him, or argued with him, or threatened to leave him. She was a noble woman and she loved him. He loved her too. And racing was his job. She couldn't expect him to leave it at fifty, while he knew he could still win.

The final days on the boat were peaceful. His phone meetings got longer, the deals more intense. He had taken a huge risk on the commodities market again, and won. He had made a killing while sitting on the boat. He loved it.

Maggie swam a lot, and she worked on her computer, contacting artists she wanted to represent. She had twelve of them now, and said she was going to keep it small at first, test the model, and not grow too fast. She wanted to keep it exclusive. He would have gone bigger and bolder, but he let her do what she thought best.

They had a romantic dinner on the boat on the last night. She looked beautiful in a white dress she had bought at Hermès in Saint Barth's when they'd stopped there. It set off her tan, and there was something so elegant and dignified about her. He thought her eyes looked sad, but she sat straight in her chair, and gazed deep into his eyes. They held hands, and made love when they went to his cabin. Afterwards, he thought he saw tears in her eyes. He didn't want to ask her again if she was all right. He thought maybe she missed Aden, or something had reminded her of Brad. She hadn't cried for Brad for a long time. Paul had no idea that she was crying for him.

They flew to New York the next day, and checked in at the Four Seasons, into one of the large suites he liked on the fiftieth floor, with a spectacular view. He had meetings at his lawyers' offices as soon as they arrived. They were flying to London the next day, and Paul was pressed for time. His lawyers congratulated him on his remarkable survival and recovery, and he smiled.

"Nine lives," he reminded them. "Hopefully ten. I'm racing next month." None of them commented. They knew him, and how he lived. Always on the edge. He was a phenomenon.

He met Maggie back at the hotel in time for dinner at La Grenouille, his favorite restaurant in New York, and now hers. She was wearing a chic black dress and her eyes looked like sapphires as she gazed at him.

"Good day?" he asked her in the car on the way to the restaurant. He was wearing a dark suit, and was very handsome. He looked well with a tan, and his silvery hair shone. He had a haircut after he met with his lawyers and was impeccable. He was in top form.

"Yes," she said quietly, as she looked out the window. It was a short distance from the hotel.

"What did you do?"

"I saw some artists downtown." She smiled at him, and he had an eerie feeling looking at her, it was as though she wasn't really there. There was an ethereal quality to her. She seemed just out of reach, like a ghost. She looked exceptionally beautiful. Heads turned as they walked into the restaurant, and every man in the restaurant recognized Paul immediately. He was a legend everywhere he went, but Maggie didn't mind. She had no desire for center stage and it suited him.

The dinner was delicious, although he noticed that Maggie ate very little.

"Are you feeling okay?" In the past two weeks he thought that she had lost weight. She looked remarkable, but he worried that she wasn't well.

"Just tired," she said. And when they went back to the hotel, they didn't make love that night. He had a call from Tokyo when they walked in, and she was asleep when he got to bed. They had a long flight to London the next day and he didn't disturb her. He turned out the light without noticing that her pillow was damp. He fell asleep instantly. It had been a good day for him and a nice evening. The call from Tokyo had been good news. He was looking forward to his meetings in London, and a race in a month. He was always a star in races in Spain, and won them impressively every year. He knew he would again. He was always brought in as the coup de grâce in a race now. His sponsors knew that he would do whatever he had to to win.

Maggie got up early and was packed when Paul got up. She ordered breakfast for him while he showered and dressed. It was waiting for him when he came to the table in a blue blazer and slacks.

"You're not eating?" He was surprised.

"I'll eat on the plane," she said quietly, and went to close her bag.

She was ready when he was, with perfect synchronicity. She never made him wait. He called for the porter to get their bags. And they were in the lobby five minutes later.

They walked to the sidewalk together, and she said something to the porter Paul didn't hear. He wasn't paying attention as the porter put her suitcase to one side, and Maggie stepped forward and hailed a cab, which startled Paul. He stared at her in surprise.

"What are you doing? We're taking a car to the airport." His bag had just been put in the trunk of the town car waiting for them. Hers wasn't.

"I'm not," she said quietly, looking deep into his eyes. "This is where I leave the circus. I'm going home. I'm not going to watch you try to kill yourself again, Paul. Canada did it for me. I thought it did it for you too, but I was wrong. Nothing is ever going to do it for you. It's never going to be enough. There's always going to be one more race, one more death-defying act you think you can pull off. One day, you're going to lose, next race, next time, some-day, and I don't want to be there to see it. I can't." And from the look on her face, he knew she meant it. She wasn't crying, but the sorrow in her eyes was worse than tears. He suddenly understood why she hadn't argued with him on the boat about the race. She must have made her decision then, or in the days since, without telling him. He knew her well but had missed all the signs.

"Maggie, please . . ." he pleaded with her. "Just let me finish out this contract. I'm getting too old for it anyway. We'll talk about it after Spain." He was begging her and she didn't move.

"No, we won't. There's nothing to talk about. You know what you want and so do I. You're not too old. You'll never be too old to want danger and risk your life." She smiled sadly at him. "But I am. I can't watch you do this again. I don't want to be there when you finally lose the bet."

"I'm not going to," he said with the certainty of a gambler, sure he would win.

"You will lose one day. I don't want to see it. And I can't do this to Aden either. He loves you. So do I. He doesn't deserve to lose another man in his life. Neither do I."

Tears filled her eyes as she opened the door of the cab then and got in. The doorman put her suitcase in the trunk as Paul gazed at her in disbelief. "You're leaving me?"

She glanced out the open cab window and nodded. "Call me when you're too old to race. I'll probably be dead by then." She told the driver to take her to LaGuardia, and they pulled away and drove off with Paul staring after them. He could barely get into the town car after she left. He was distraught.

An hour later, he was at Teterboro airport in New Jersey, and boarded his plane. He barely spoke to the steward and settled into his seat. There were tears sliding down his cheeks when they took off for London. Maggie had just gotten on her flight to Chicago. She had a text from Paul but didn't read it. It didn't matter what he said now. She was done. She had seen him through races and an avalanche and his life-and-death battle with the IRS. Her mother had told her at seventeen that he'd be trouble, and she was right. And no matter how much she loved him, she couldn't let him destroy her life, and she knew he would. She erased his text without reading it, and turned off her phone. She closed her eyes, and could feel the pain of peeling him away from her soul. But whatever it took, she was finished. Paul would have to do his dance with death on his own. She couldn't watch it anymore, or live it with him.

She picked up her bag in Chicago and hailed a cab at the curb. When she got home, she turned her phone on. She had four more messages from Paul and erased them all without reading them. She had heard everything he had to say. She was done.

Chapter 17

Maggie felt empty when she got home. She didn't want to talk to anyone or see anyone. She didn't want to tell Helen she was there. She needed time to herself, to heal and come back. She knew she had to do it herself this time, without help. Nobody could do this except she herself. She had to bury him now. He was dead to her, as he had been for thirty years before she'd found him again.

She sent Aden a text so he'd know where she was, but she didn't tell him what she'd done. She knew he'd be devastated that she'd left Paul, but she had done it to save her own life, and even her son's. Paul Gilmore was a dangerous man to love. A heartbreaker of the worst kind. She couldn't afford him in her life.

She took long walks for the first week she was home. The text messages continued, but she kept erasing them, and after another week, they stopped. He realized that she wasn't coming back. She was a remarkable woman, and he didn't deserve her. He knew that now. And if she wanted her freedom, he owed her at least that. She had brought him back from the dead, and he had broken her heart in exchange. He understood what she wanted and needed, and he couldn't give it to her. Worse, he didn't want to. He wanted racing more than he wanted her, and she knew it. He hated himself for it, but he couldn't let go of what the races meant to him. They meant he was a winner, that death couldn't conquer him, that he was afraid of nothing, and dying meant nothing to him. He was the bravest and the toughest and the strongest, the most fearless man alive. He had been so frightened as a little boy, when his father left them penniless, and later when his mother died. He had fought fear from then on, and won every time, or close enough.

But in the end, Maggie was stronger than he was. He was terrified without her now.

After she'd been back a week, she contacted the artists she'd been meeting with, launched the website, and contacted everyone on her extensive mailing list. The site featured a slideshow of the artists' works that she was offering. Within days, she had inquiries and responses, and four clients eager to buy some of the work she was representing. She made her first sale two weeks after she'd launched, and felt stronger by then. She'd spoken to Aden and told him that she had left Paul. He was sad, but he said he understood, and he hoped they'd see him again one day.

"If he's still alive," she said, and sounded angrier than she wanted to. She wasn't angry, she was sad too, and disappointed. He had lied while almost dying was fresh in his mind. But as soon as he recovered, he was back in the game.

Aden said he'd come home for spring break in March, since she wouldn't be in London now. She had no plans to return to Europe, and no reason to go there. She hated to admit it, but she would miss the boat. Who wouldn't? It was a little taste of heaven on earth, and she'd been happy with Paul. She loved him, but she knew she wouldn't one day. She had forgotten him before, and would again.

She'd been back for three weeks when she let Helen know she was home, and told her simply that she had left Paul, and it was better this way.

"Should I ask what happened?"

"It doesn't matter. It never should have happened at all. He was a fantasy from my youth."

"I'm sorry, Maggie."

"Me too." She told Helen about the online gallery then. She had finally done it, and was proud of herself.

She picked up the threads of her life, the ordinary pleasures she had enjoyed when she lived there. She had stopped living a life there ever since Brad died and the fateful trip to Europe where she met Paul again. It had been all about him ever since. Now it had to be about her again, or maybe for the first time in her life. She was going to have to do this alone, and figure out where she wanted to live. Chicago or Lake Forest or maybe New York. She could do whatever she wanted. It was frightening, but exciting too. Missing Paul was like a dull ache, a phantom limb, and she would have to get used to that. They had been together for a year and a half, and it was over now. She knew she'd survive, no matter how painful at first.

She was looking at slides of new work for her online gallery when Aden called her one week later on a Saturday. She was happy to hear him, but he sounded agitated.

"Turn your TV on, Mom." His voice was unusually sharp. "Now!"

"Why?"

"Just turn it on. The sports channel, or a news channel. I think it'll be all over the place."

"Is he dead? I don't want to see it." She suddenly knew why he had called.

"Just turn it on," he insisted. Reluctantly she did.

She could see a racetrack in the distance and hear a Spanish announcer behind the two American commentators speaking. They were engaged in a rapid-fire exchange, as though something incredible had happened. One of them was a famous retired race car driver, and the other was a network anchor they used for major sports events.

"I don't want to see this, Aden," she said firmly.

"Just listen, Mom." She was about to turn it off when something stopped her, and a photograph of Paul filled the screen briefly. Maybe he had died, and she should know. But the commentators were still talking and the crowd was screaming Paul's name. There were no ambulances visible, so maybe he wasn't dead or injured.

She watched, curious about what was going on. Both commentators were excited and the network anchor spoke to the audience almost breathlessly. "For those of you just tuning in, we've just seen racing history here. Neither of us have ever seen anything like this before, have we, Pete?" he asked the retired driver, who said he hadn't. The crowd seemed to be screaming louder. She wondered if someone had killed someone on the track. "We've just seen one of the most famous Formula One drivers in history withdraw from the race minutes before it started, 'for personal reasons.' He was lost in the snow for four days after an avalanche in Canada three months ago, we're wondering if it had something to do with that. This would have been his first race since the accident. He was in the pit, checking his car an hour before the race, and all we know, folks, is that he walked off, announced that he was forfeiting the race, and then left a letter confirming it.

"He'll be fined for forfeiting at the last minute, which he was certainly aware of. He's been known for his 'risk everything, I dare you, winner takes all' attitude for thirty years of racing, but this beats everything. His sponsor can withdraw his contract for this. Paul Gilmore, where are you? The crowd has been going crazy here. You can hear them behind us. No one seems to know what those 'personal reasons' are. He's been unavailable for comment, and word is he left the track minutes ago. For those of you watching at home, this is a first, and a shocker coming from a legend like Paul Gilmore. We've all seen him race, even with broken bones." They were still talking when Aden spoke to her on the phone she was holding.

"I think he withdrew for you, Mom." He knew why she had left him. "He's going to pay a big fine for this."

"He can afford it," she said coldly. "Maybe he's sick. He does what he wants, and maybe he doesn't want them to know. Maybe his feet went numb again and he couldn't drive."

"I don't think so. It would take something pretty damn important for him to forfeit a race. He's never done that before. He's too big for that." She didn't disagree with him, but wasn't going to guess about it. The announcers were still trying to figure it out. They were hinting at a mental breakdown of some kind when she turned it off.

She was curious but didn't want to text and ask him. She didn't want to open Pandora's box again. Whatever his reason for forfeiting, it must have been a good one. It was noon for her then, and she went about her day, then went back to the emails she was writing to the artists whose work she was selling.

She bought groceries after, and had just scrambled some eggs at eight o'clock that night when she heard a text come in. She was going to ignore it, but thought it might be Aden, and that he had heard more about Paul. Instead she saw it was from Paul himself. She was about to erase it without reading, when curiosity got the best of her and she opened it and stared at what it said.

"I just flew here from Madrid. I'm in Chicago. I retired today."

"Why?" she texted back.

"I figure I may have used up the ninth life in Canada and decided to quit while I'm ahead. And I'm in Chicago because you live here and I love you. I did it for you, Maggie, if you still care." She didn't know what to answer, and had tears in her eyes. She didn't want to care, but she still did. She didn't trust him. He'd find some other way to risk his life if he wasn't racing. Skydiving. Mountain climbing. He'd find something. He couldn't help himself.

He had spent the last four weeks thinking about her, and trying to decide what to do. And when he got to the racetrack that morning, it all became clear. It was so simple. He just had to do it. It had been easier than he'd thought it would be.

"You probably don't believe me," he texted her when she didn't respond. "I wouldn't either. I could have won the race. You mean more to me. My sponsor will probably sue me for walking, but I don't give a damn. I flew here to see you. Can I come home?" Her eggs were stone cold as she stared at her phone. She didn't want to go through it with him again. Canada had almost killed her. But what if he really did it for her?

"I'm here," was all she responded, and forty minutes later, her doorbell rang. She opened the door and he was standing there, still in his driving suit. He hadn't bothered to change on the plane.

He looked serious when she opened the door to him, and so did she. She stood there, staring at him.

"You made history today," she said to him, still not sure what to think or if she believed him. But it had been on TV.

"I know," he said, and then gently pulled her into his arms. "I did it for you," he told her again.

"So you said." She had left him standing on the sidewalk outside the Four Seasons a month before and she believed it was the right thing to do. But she couldn't ignore what he'd just done in

Spain, whether it was for her or not. It was huge for him to have done it, and took incredible courage. He'd been racing cars since he was a kid, and was one of the most famous drivers in the world. "Thank you," she said softly. And then he kissed her and she looked at him in surprise. The man who had nine lives had come home. "Why did you do it?" she asked him when he stopped.

"I have too much to lose now. You and Aden. I don't want to lose you, Maggie." She nodded. She didn't want to lose him either. They had lost each other the first time at seventeen and eighteen, and neither of them wanted it to happen again more than thirty years later. Something had brought them together the first time, and again now. She didn't know if it was kismet or fate, or an accident of some kind, but it was stronger than they were. And she knew his passion for danger. But he had walked away from a race for her. And if he could do that, she could take a chance on him. She knew as she looked at him that she was willing to risk it, and brave enough to try.

He followed her into the living room and they sat down on the couch in the small simple house she had outgrown. And as she looked at him, she saw in her mind's eye the boy who had biked away when she was eighteen with a wave and a smile. She remembered him distinctly and she put her arms around the boy and the man and held him close to her.

"Welcome home," she said softly, and he kissed her again. She realized then that her mother had been wrong. Sometimes the wild ones are worth the wait, and don't break your heart after all.

About the Author

DANIELLE STEEL has been hailed as one of the world's best-selling authors, with almost a billion copies of her novels sold. Her many international bestsellers include *The Affair, Finding Ashley, Neighbors, All That Glitters, Royal, Daddy's Girls, The Wedding Dress,* and other highly acclaimed novels. She is also the author of *His Bright Light,* the story of her son Nick Traina's life and death; *A Gift of Hope,* a memoir of her work with the homeless; *Expect a Miracle,* a book of her favorite quotations for inspiration and comfort; *Pure Joy,* about the dogs she and her family have loved; and the children's books *Pretty Minnie in Paris* and *Pretty Minnie in Hollywood.*

daniellesteel.com
Facebook.com/DanielleSteelOfficial
Twitter: @daniellesteel
Instagram: @OfficialDanielleSteel

About the Type

This book was set in Charter, a typeface designed in 1987 by Matthew Carter (b. 1937) for Bitstream, Inc., a digital type-foundry that he cofounded in 1981. One of the most influential typographers of our time, Carter designed this versatile font to feature a compact width, squared serifs, and open letterforms. These features give the typeface a fresh, highly legible, and unencumbered appearance.